# GREETINGS
# FROM
# PLANET
# EARTH

D1015957

## BARBARA KERLEY

### SCHOLASTIC INC.
New York Toronto London Auckland
Sydney Mexico City New Delhi Hong Kong

This book was originally published in hardcover by Scholastic Press in 2007.

ISBN 978-0-439-80204-8

12 11 10 9 8 7 6 5 4 3 2 1    10 11 12 13 14 15/0

Printed in the U.S.A. 40
First Scholastic paperback printing,
September 2010

Illustrations copyright © 2007 by Istvan Banyai
The illustration type was set in BaseNine SmallCaps
The text type was set in Futura Book,
Futura BookOblique, Bancroft Book Italic, and
BaseTwelve Sans • Book design by Marijka Kostiw

Many thanks . . .

To Ronald B. Frankum of The Vietnam Archive, Texas Tech University, for answering my many questions about servicemen training and tours of duty; and to Susan K. Mordan of the Library of Congress, for details about LOC displays in 1977.

To my amazing editor, Tracy Mack, for being so darn smart and for knowing when to push harder and when to wrap me up in a warm blanket; to Marijka Kostiw, for her creative vision; to Anne Dunn, for her insightful reading; and to Leslie Budnick and Abby Ranger for their unflagging enthusiasm and support.

To my agent, Jodi Reamer, for her great energy and sense of humor.

To my writing buddies, Mary Nethery, Pamela F. Service, Natasha Wing, Ellen Dee Davidson, Kim T. Griswell, Deborah Heiligman, Gennifer Choldenko, and Martha Longshore, for all they have taught me.

To my mom, for reading to me, and my dad, for sharing his love of history.

And to Scott and Anna, for living with me every day and loving me anyway.

To Uncle Ed,

Aunt Ruth,

and the families

who put up

with them:

Kathi, Jeffrey,

Steven, and Allison;

Bill and Laura

# CONTENTS

MARE TRANQUILLITATIS —
SEA OF TRANQUILITY 5

RIMA GALILAEI —
GALILEO'S RILLE 23

RUPES MERCATOR —
MERCATOR'S FAULT 95

MARE COGNITUM —
KNOWN SEA 129

EINSTEIN  205


LACUS AESTATIS —
    SUMMER LAKE  227



SOURCES AND SUGGESTIONS
    FOR FURTHER READING  244

# MOM SAYS I HAVE MY HEAD IN THE

clouds, but she's a hundred miles short.

JeeBee says, "Stars in his eyes."

Janet just calls me a space cadet.

It's even worse now because NASA's launching Voyager 2 this summer: August 20, 1977.

Last night at dinner Janet said, "Let's send Theodore to Florida so he can sneak onto that rocket. I'll donate my allowance."

She's a crack-up, that Janet.

Voyager 1 takes off after Voyager 2 because 1 travels faster. It will get to Jupiter sooner.

But even though Voyager 2 is slower, it's still my favorite: It blasts off first, with nothing to keep it company, sailing into deep, dark space all by itself.

I know that sounds dumb. I know a rocket can't really be brave or lonely. But still . . .

1

It will fly past Jupiter and Saturn, all the way to Uranus and Neptune. Janet has a joke about that, too. "You know why it's going to Ur-a-nus, Theodore? 'Cause you're a pain in the butt."

She's a real crack-up, alright. You don't know what you're missing.

Oh. Uh, I didn't mean that....

I mean —

Sorry. This is just ... so hard. I don't know how to talk to you.

And using a tape recorder feels weird. Like I can hear my voice all by itself, in my empty room, and no matter how quietly I talk, it's still too loud.

But I want to tell you who I am.

My science teacher asked our class if what we do is the same as who we are. At first I thought, sure. Someone who teaches is a teacher. Someone who fixes cars is a mechanic. Someone who fights is a soldier.

But I don't think that anymore. I think sometimes we do things that aren't who we are at all. And the more that happens, the harder it is to find yourself again.

I decided when I started this tape that I would say whatever I was thinking. I'm afraid if I say something you don't like, I'll lose you.

Though I'm not even sure if I want you.

But I guess if you get mad about anything, you could stop listening for a while. Just don't stop completely, or you won't get to hear how it ends.

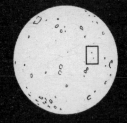

MARE TRANQUILLITATIS

# SEA OF TRANQUILITY

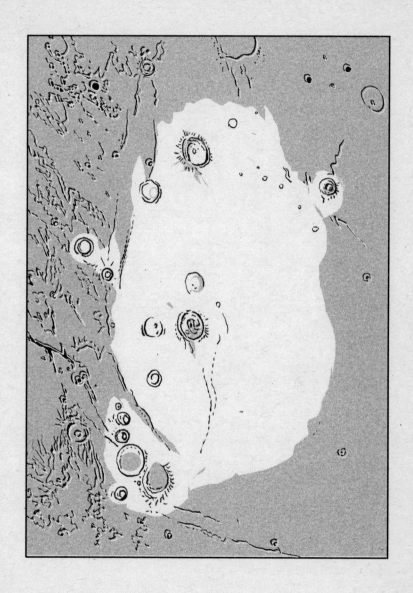

# THEO WAS DIGGING IT: THEY

were supposed to be talking about cells — that was the chapter they were on in their science book — but Mr. Meyer had spent the whole period talking about space. He paced in front of the class, his glasses glinting, his thick brown mustache wiggling as he talked. "The *Voyager* probes will have a special feature, something that's never been on a spacecraft before."

"A McDonald's?" Kenny asked, shooting Theo a glance.

Theo grinned. His best friend was a doofus — a big, lumbering goofball with a mouthful of braces that sometimes had a little lunch stuck in them.

"No," Mr. Meyer said. "The spacecraft are *unmanned*, remember?"

Three hands shot up — three girls' hands, Theo noticed.

"Sorry," Mr. Meyer said. "Un*personed*."

The hands went back down.

"Each spacecraft is going to carry a golden record: a message, in pictures and sounds, from Earth to any aliens out there in space." He stroked his tie, dark blue with stars, and his eyes traveled around the room until they finally rested on Theo. Mr. Meyer smiled. "And that's where this assignment comes in. . . ."

He explained: The class was going to create its own message from Earth. Each kid would get to put up one picture on the bulletin board and add one minute to a class tape recording. One picture and one minute, to share what they thought was most important about Earth.

"But how are we supposed to choose?" Theo asked.

"That's up to you to figure out," Mr. Meyer answered. "Think about what Earth is, what earthlings are like. What would someone from another planet need to know to understand us? Look around you — what do you think is most important?"

"The best thing on Earth — that's easy!" Kenny said to Theo as they walked out of school together. "Pizza!"

"So that's your plan?" Theo nudged Kenny with his shoulder. Kenny was so tall that Theo's shoulder hit Kenny's bicep. "You're going to staple a slice of pizza to the bulletin board?"

Before Kenny could answer, a voice called, "Kenny! You have an orthodontist appointment, remember?" Kenny's mom stood by her car in the parking lot. She gave Theo a big wave. "Happy birthday, Theo!" she called before sliding into the driver's seat.

"Thanks!" Theo waved back. Then he reminded Kenny, "Come by after dinner for some cake."

"Okay." Kenny hoofed it to his car.

Theo's stomach rumbled as he walked home — he was always hungry after school. Tonight there'd be birthday cake. Cake was good, very good, but the best thing on Earth was definitely a cheeseburger, fries, and a chocolate shake.

Theo stopped walking. He had spare change left over from lunch. Not enough for a whole meal, but he could get some fries. What a great excuse! He could buy the fries, take a picture of them, and then eat them — *and* call it homework!

He hurried down the road to a fast-food joint, the salty smell of burgers pulling him through the door. He placed his order. He ate one, just one crisp hot French fry, and then rolled up the bag.

Theo jogged home, plunked his books and the fries down on the kitchen counter, and ran upstairs. Where was that stupid camera? He searched his desk, under his bed, on the floor of the closet, beneath shoes and dirty socks. . . . There! On the bookcase!

He grabbed the camera and raced downstairs into the kitchen and smack into Janet. She was leaning against the counter, shoving the last fries into her mouth. "Hey there, birthday boy," she said, crushing the bag.

"Janet!"

"What?" She wiped her mouth with the back of her hand.

"You ate my fries!"

"Oh, were those yours?"

"I was going to take a picture of them!" He explained about the project, the message from Earth —

But Janet cut him off. "Think with your *brain*, not your *stomach*. Do you honestly believe that French fries are the most important thing about Earth?" She patted his shoulder on the way out. "Trust me, I did you a favor." She burped. "You should thank me, Theodore."

**SCIENCE IS MY FAVORITE CLASS IN**
school, partly because of my teacher, Mr. Meyer.

He listens to me. He doesn't lie, either.

I haven't told him the truth about you. Not exactly. Mom wouldn't want me to. She likes to keep things private, and she sees him at school. But when he asks me if something's wrong, I don't want to say no. It's my secret, too, not just Mom's. I should be able to tell who I want.

I love his class because it's full of stuff I can't stop thinking about. Like the Voyager probes. Each one is going to have a gold-plated record. Thousands of years from now, some space creature may play the record and hear voices, plus music and sounds like birds chirping. And there'll be pictures of people and animals.

NASA had to decide what to call the probes. They were thinking maybe Discovery 1 and 2, but they chose Voyager instead. That's better, I think, because the probes travel so far, and the trip will take such a long time. Besides, it's not just what they discover that matters, it's the golden record, too. It's what they bring with them.

Mr. Meyer said it's like reaching across the galaxy to shake hands.

**THEO SAW THE RED PACKAGE,**
saw it but reached for something else.

"Happy birthday, honey." His mom smiled, but Theo could tell she was nervous by the way she looked at the other presents as if they were going to bite her. He read the card: "Happy Birthday, Theo! Love, Mom." There was a bundle of dollar bills, too — twelve, he knew. His mom always gave him a dollar for every year.

He tore striped paper off the soft package. A Washington Redskins jersey. "I noticed your old one is getting a little tight across the shoulders," she said.

"It's great, Mom. Thanks."

The smallest package was from Janet, wrapped in toilet paper with a big pink bow stuck on top. The card said, "Make sure you *recycle* the wrapper, baby brother."

He pulled on the toilet paper and the present unrolled itself. A small white tube bounced out onto the tabletop. Pimple cream. "You *are* twelve now, Theodore," Janet said. "You're *bound* to get a pimple soon." Janet was two years older than Theo and spent a lot of time in the beauty supply section of the drugstore, *and* in the bathroom.

"Honestly, Janet," JeeBee scolded.

Janet flipped her hair back and laughed. It was streaky blond, even though Theo and his mom's were brown. Whatever Janet did to hers took hours.

"Never mind about pimples, Theo." JeeBee pushed the last two packages across the table to him. She was so short that her tummy almost touched the tabletop as she leaned over. "Happy birthday!"

Again, he avoided the red one and reached instead for the bigger one, wrapped in shiny gold. JeeBee's presents were the best. She wasn't like some grandmas, giving slippers or pajamas. He opened the card: "A handy map for your arrival. Love, JeeBee."

He hefted the present, an inch thick, then slid off the wrapping.

Incredible.

An atlas of the moon.

Theo had studied the moon's best-known features through his binoculars: the Sea of Tranquility, where *Apollo 11* landed and the first footprints still lay in moon dust. Copernicus, a crater so huge it appeared on Galileo's map in 1610. The Ocean of Storms, filled not with water but with dark, smooth lava cooled millions of years ago.

But this book had page after page of close-ups: Thousands of craters. Whole mountain ranges. Every sea, every bay, every rille and wrinkle ridge, each with its own name. The face of the moon — blotchy, pockmarked, beautiful.

"Wow. Talk about pimples," Janet said, peering over his shoulder.

Theo ignored her. The features were in Latin — *mare* for sea, *lacus* for lake — and now Theo saw that every crater was named after someone. He recognized some of the names: Pythagoras, da Vinci, even Hercules. But there were hundreds Theo had never heard of: Cuvier, one of the founders of paleontology. Porter, an architect who designed huge telescopes. Marinus, a geographer from the second century. The book talked about each one.

Theo looked at his grandma and smiled. "I love it."

JeeBee shrugged. "Of course, it's just the *map*. You'll have to chart your own course one day when you get there."

Theo nodded and turned the pages. Maybe if he kept reading, he wouldn't have to open the red present.

But JeeBee pushed it a little closer. "One more," she said.

Theo looked at Mom. Her head was bowed so low

that Theo couldn't even see her face, just her puffy brown hair. He glanced at Janet.

She had her hands crossed in front of her chest. "Oh, just open it." But then her voice softened a bit. "It's okay, Theo."

He nodded and picked up the present, a little red envelope taped on top.

The card was never signed. It always said the same thing: "Happy Birthday." Theo didn't even bother to open it. He ripped off the wrapping paper with a quick, tearing sound.

Inside was a model kit, this time for a *Saturn 5* rocket and launchpad. "Wow," Theo said. He never knew who to thank, exactly, so he never exactly said "thank you." But he always looked at JeeBee.

"Let me take some pictures," she said, suddenly busy.

"Wait!" Janet cried. "I need my hairbrush. . . ." She ran upstairs.

Mom brought over the cake, then went looking for matches.

JeeBee gathered up the cards and handed Theo the red envelope. "You missed one."

Theo sighed. But when he opened the card, his breath caught in his throat.

This time the card *was* signed: "Happy Birthday, from your dad." It was JeeBee's handwriting, but still . . .

Theo flushed. He slipped the cards into his lap.

Mom lit the candles, her lips pressed together in a hard, tight line. Janet came down, brushing her hair and murmuring her version of the birthday song: ". . . you look like a monkey, and you smell like one, too. . . ."

JeeBee fiddled the camera out of its case. "Put on your jersey, Theo."

"And some pimple cream," Janet added. "A big blob on the tip of your nose. Here, let me help you."

Theo swatted her away. He pulled the Redskins jersey over his shirt and stood the book up on the table, cover facing toward JeeBee.

She put the camera to her eye. "Say 'cheese'!"

Janet grabbed the tube of pimple cream and held it next to Theo's head. Mom stood beside them, shoulders slumped, her arms hanging at her sides. Theo hesitated, then picked up the model rocket kit and held it in his hand, feeling his lips quiver as he forced them into a smile.

When Kenny came over later, he and Theo dug into the rest of the cake. Mom never let Theo eat that many sweets, but he knew he'd get away with it on his birthday.

He and Kenny were just starting their second pieces when Janet sauntered in. "Good evening, Kenneth. Enjoying your snack?"

Theo watched the blush spread over Kenny's face until even his ears were bright pink.

Janet pulled a glass from the cupboard. "How about some nice cold milk to go with that?" She filled the glass and set it down by Kenny.

He hunched over his plate and kept eating.

"Hey, I want some milk, too," Theo said.

But Janet just put her hands on her hips and *tsk*ed. "Theodore, how can Kenneth enjoy his snack if he doesn't have a napkin?" She placed one by Kenny's plate and then sat down right next to him.

Kenny stuffed the rest of his cake into his mouth. He pushed back from the table so quickly his chair fell over.

"Better bring that napkin along," Janet said as he bolted from the room. "You have frosting on your chin!"

Theo set the chair back on its legs, drained Kenny's glass of milk, and cleared the dishes. Janet laughed the whole time.

"Geez, Janet," Theo said.

"Hey, all I did was sit down next to him." She shrugged. "He's the one who freaked out."

Theo found Kenny upstairs, at his desk, twisting model pieces of the *Saturn 5* rocket off the plastic frames and dropping them in a little pile. "Wait, Kenny! You're bunching everything up!" If the pieces got mixed up, it was almost impossible to figure out how the model fit together. Theo sat down next to him. "Sorry about Janet. I think she likes bugging you."

Kenny shuddered. "Yeah." He stood, still antsy, and started playing with the other models — planes, rockets, even a helicopter that hung from the ceiling by strings. Theo could barely reach them, but Kenny batted them around easily, making them fly in crazy circles.

Theo spread the instructions out on his desk. He knew he'd built the first model with his dad, though he didn't really remember doing it. Then, after his dad left, JeeBee helped with the next three. The last three he'd built with Kenny. There were seven in all, one for every year since Theo's fifth birthday.

Kenny flopped down on the bed. "I don't get it. How does he give you a present if he's not here?"

"Shh!" Theo jumped up and closed the door. "JeeBee

buys them. Every year we know it's supposed to be from my dad, but no one *says* it's from him — we never talk about it."

Talking about it would be against the rules. Mom had never told Theo what the rules were, but he'd figured them out. Number One: If you *pretend* everything is fine, then everything *is* fine. And Number Two: Don't talk about Dad. Ever. "It's like JeeBee wants me to remember him" — he glanced at the red birthday card, lying on his desk — "but my mom doesn't."

"Why would she want you to forget him?"

Theo shook his head and sat back down. "She always has. From the start."

"From the start of what?"

"From when . . ." Theo wasn't sure how to explain it. From when he had to start being careful about what he said? From when there started being more and more things he wasn't even supposed to *notice*? "From when he was supposed to come home," Theo finally said.

He and Kenny were already friends that summer, the summer before second grade, when they were seven. "For weeks I asked my mom when he'd get here. She said she didn't know. Then one day she yelled, 'I don't know, Theo! Quit asking me!'" He swallowed around the lump in his throat. "So I asked my grandma."

Kenny sat up. "What did she say?"

For a minute Theo couldn't speak, his throat was cinched so tight. He was surprised he could still breathe. Carefully he matched the pieces of the model to the diagram, waiting until he could get the words out. He remembered exactly what JeeBee had said:

"'Your dad *wants* to come home, but he can't.'"

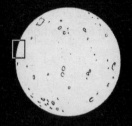

RIMA GALILAEI

# GALILEO'S RILLE

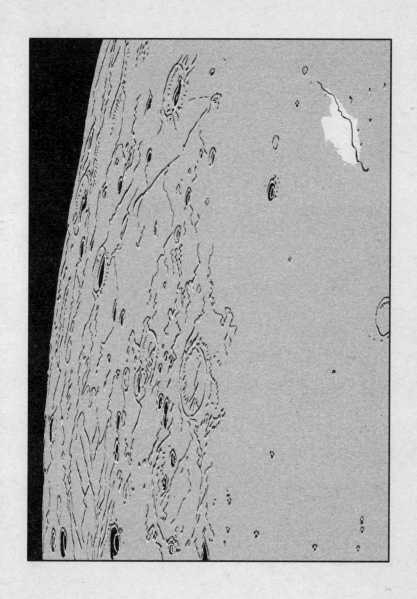

## ASTRONAUT MEANS SOMEONE WHO

sails to the stars. I wonder what the stars would look like up close?

A lot of things in space are different than they seem. From here the stars in a constellation look like they're all together in a group, but really they're not. Like Orion. His shoulders look like they're right over his belt, but if you got close enough, you'd see that one shoulder is millions of miles farther on.

If you sailed to Orion's belt and looked around, you'd probably see different constellations. Instead of a crab or a lion, maybe a peacock or a crocodile, or even an elephant.

I used to think you could make up your own constellations.

Sometimes when I look at the stars, I get this excited feeling: I'm part of something bigger. I almost can't stand being in my body — like if I could just figure a way to get out of my skin, I'd be up there, too. When I was little, I used to jump.

It's easy to talk to you about space. Well, not easy. Easier. I don't even know if you care about space. But I said I was going to tell you who I am, and that's part of it.

Besides, even if you don't care about space, maybe you care about me.

# "SO," MR. MEYER SAID TO THE

class the next day, "did anyone finish their *Voyager* assignment overnight?"

Everyone shook their heads.

"Don't worry. It's not due for two weeks." He laughed. "I thought I'd get the discussion rolling with a simple question." He walked over to an empty bulletin board and tacked up a piece of paper: WHO ARE WE? He turned to the class, straightened his toucan tie, and waited.

Theo looked at the other kids in the room. No one said anything.

Finally Kenny raised his hand. "We are the Tigers — the mighty, mighty Tigers?"

The class laughed. Mr. Meyer smiled. "Thanks for the school spirit, Kenny." Then, to the class, he asked, "So, is that how you see yourselves, first and foremost: as members of this school?"

"No way, this school is bogus," Rhonda complained. She reminded Theo of Janet.

"Besides," Theo added, "we're graduating in a few weeks."

"Good point, Theo," Mr. Meyer said. "Our allegiances change all the time. Next year you'll be at the junior high. So who are you? Virginians? Americans?"

"Aren't those the same thing?" Cynthia asked.

Mr. Meyer smiled. "Are they? How about the bigger picture? Are you the same as a kid in, say, China? How about a kid in Ethiopia?"

Theo shrugged. "We're all kids."

"And are people the same, all over the world?" Mr. Meyer tapped the piece of paper. "Who are we?"

Theo and Kenny talked about it as they tossed a football in Kenny's big backyard after school. Kenny said in a robotic, alien voice: "We are earthlings. We play football."

"Shouldn't you sound like a human —"

But Kenny interrupted him, in the same mechanical voice: "What is that strange brown thing, made from the skin of a pig?"

"Is that what you're going to do for your tape?" Theo lobbed a high one. "Talk about football like a weird alien?"

"What is weird about this voice? I must vaporize you now." Kenny threw the football, hard.

Theo barely caught it. "Seriously: football?" He rubbed his hand on his jeans to take away the sting. "The most important thing on Earth?"

"Well, yeah," Kenny said, the robot voice abandoned. "A picture of the Redskins. And a play-by-play for the tape — the Redskins coming from behind to win." He flashed a victory sign. "Hey, can we use your tape recorder?"

Theo threw the football. "I don't know. I'll have to ask my mom tonight."

Kenny's back door opened. His mom stuck her head out the door. "Kenny, time to set the table for dinner. It's almost five-thirty, Theo."

"Thanks." Theo's mom didn't like it when he was late. Family dinner started at six o'clock, and she wanted everyone there.

Theo waved bye to Kenny and walked through the gate to the front yard, where his bike lay on the grass. He climbed on and started pedaling home. Football. Theo liked football. But the most important thing on Earth? Choosing football seemed kind of like choosing French fries.

Mr. Meyer had said to look around. If he hurried, Theo could do a little exploring and still make it home in half an hour. He kept on riding to the edge of town.

There was a new subdivision going up about a mile from his house. The house frames looked like skeletons. Theo breathed in the sweet smell of just-cut wood.

For weeks he'd watched construction workers pound and saw, tromping around in muddy boots, tools hanging from their leather belts. But they'd all left for the day. Theo leaned his bike against a stack of two-by-fours. He slipped in through a gap in the framing and explored a house on foot, figuring out what kind of room each space would become.

To build a house from the ground up: That was really something.

As Theo rode home, he thought it through. Human beings built things. Maybe that was what Mr. Meyer was getting at. WHO ARE WE? We're builders.

Theo decided he could take a picture of a house being built. Now all he had to figure out was what sound to record for the tape.

Five minutes later he wheeled his bike into the garage and parked it next to the two other bikes against the wall: Janet's, bright red with silver streamers on the handlebars — she'd gotten it for her eleventh birthday, though she never rode it anymore. And his dad's, black and beginning to rust, its tires flat.

There weren't many traces of his dad in the house, Theo realized, just some photos in an album and a few books that had his name written on the inside flap. But when Theo looked around the garage, he saw his dad everywhere, from the faded backpack hanging on the wall to the workbench. Especially the workbench.

His dad must have made it years ago. It was a big table in the corner of the garage, with sturdy four-by-fours for legs and a smooth, particleboard top. His dad's tools hung neatly on pegs on the wall: saws and wrenches, pliers and screwdrivers. On top of the bench were little boxes of screws and a big jar of nails.

But what Theo liked best was the hammer — heavy and solid. Years ago he'd buried a stray block of wood under the bench, in a big box of greasy rags. He pulled it out whenever he felt like pounding something, and when it became too full of nails, he'd taken another one. He had four pieces of wood hidden in the box now, each embedded with dozens and dozens of nails.

Theo crossed the garage and opened the door to the kitchen. He could smell hamburgers cooking. The timer was beeping, but Janet just sat at the kitchen table, talking right over it. "Twenty-six problems! He only gave us ten minutes and said we had to finish at home!"

JeeBee emerged from behind the refrigerator door, holding milk and mayonnaise and a big bottle of ketchup. "I expect that's why it's called 'homework,' dear." She winked at Theo. "Get the timer, could you, Theo?"

As soon as he saw JeeBee, he remembered the red birthday card. He'd been wanting to ask her about it, but how did you bring up the one thing no one was supposed to talk about?

"Could you two set the table?" JeeBee said.

"Sure." Janet didn't get up. "I mean, maybe *he* doesn't have a social life, but the *rest* of us do!"

Theo got plates and silverware as JeeBee took Tater Tots out of the oven. She'd signed the card "from your dad."

". . . like anyone *cares* about algebra, anyway . . ."

Theo filled two glasses with milk as JeeBee stirred mayonnaise into the carrot-raisin salad. She must want him to say something, he thought. But what?

". . . like when we're *dead* we're going to *care* that a-squared minus b-squared equals c-squared . . ."

"Plus b-squared," JeeBee said, dishing up the plates.

"Plus. Minus. It's my *life* we're talking about here. *My* life that *he's* wasting."

They all sat down and waited. Family dinnertime was important to Mom. When she was running late, she called JeeBee from school and asked her to come over to cook.

Theo glanced at the clock, the hands inching toward six o'clock. He only had a few minutes till Mom got home. He took a deep breath. "I started working on my model."

JeeBee gave him a big smile. "I'm glad."

"Gosh, that's just *so exciting!*" Janet looked at her plate and said, "Theodore, do you want to take a picture of these Tater Tots before I eat them?"

"I'm gluing the rocket tonight," Theo went on.

Janet picked up her fork. "I'm not eating yet," she said to JeeBee. "I'm just getting ready to eat." She dug her fork into her carrot-raisin salad and picked out a raisin. "Eeuw." She picked out another one.

"I'm saving the birthday cards," Theo said.

JeeBee smiled again. "Good."

"Eeuw." Janet pushed the raisins into a little pile on her plate, one by one. "Eeuw."

"Oh, for heaven sakes, Janet!" JeeBee cried. "They're not *bugs!* You like raisins, I know you do. I've seen you eat them before."

"They're *gross!* They're covered with *mayonnaise!*"

"But you like mayonnaise, too," JeeBee continued. "You put it on your sandwiches."

"Sometimes she just eats it out of the jar," Theo added.

Janet flicked a raisin at him. Then she grabbed the glass ketchup bottle, flipped it over, and started whacking on the bottom of it, pounding a puddle of ketchup onto her plate.

She must not be on one of her weird diets, Theo thought. Some weeks it was mostly lettuce and chocolate. Some weeks it was all yogurt and Juicy Fruit gum. He turned back to JeeBee. "I put the cards in a safe place."

"Get over yourself, Theodore," Janet groused. "Your birthday was *yesterday*, remember?"

The kitchen door opened and Theo's mom blew in, a stack of papers in her arms. "If I have to read *one more* report on ancient Greece, I'm going to *scream*. Sorry I'm late."

Theo's mom taught sixth-grade social studies, though she wasn't Theo's teacher. She said that would be a bad idea, and Theo agreed. He thought it was weird how she sometimes had to work till dinnertime since the kids left school at three-thirty. Occasionally she even had to work on Saturdays. Kenny's mom was always home. Theo liked it better when his mom was, too.

Mom washed her hands. "Thanks, Bernadette, this smells great." She called JeeBee different things, depending on . . . well, Theo didn't know depending on what.

When he'd been little, he couldn't say "Grandma Bernadette," so Janet shortened it to "G.B." Which was "JeeBee" when you said it out loud, and so now they usually just called her that.

But sometimes Theo's mom called her "Bernadette," and sometimes even "Mom," which surprised Theo because JeeBee was his dad's mom. Theo's mom's parents had both died years ago, and his dad's dad had died before Theo was even born. JeeBee was the only grandparent he and Janet had.

Mom sat down and smiled. "So, how was school?"

Janet started complaining about her dorky English teacher, her birdbrained science teacher, and the total moron who called himself a track coach. She said she had no idea where he'd gotten his degree, probably Pinhead College, or maybe Stupid U. "The guy's a *menace*." Her fork swept through the air. "He's got us running wind sprints for hours, and if our time isn't fast enough, he has us do it again!"

"Maybe he just wants you to get better," Theo said.

Janet shot him an eat-lima-beans-and-die look and

continued ranting. Theo zoned her out and thought about the *Voyager* project: a minute of sound and a single picture to capture what he thought was most important about Earth. When he took a picture of the new houses, should he bring the tape player along? He could record the men hammering. Or maybe he should tape something better. Music, or a bird chirping? He'd never thought about Earth sounds before.

". . . a complete idiot!" Janet's voice interrupted his thoughts. "We have our last track meet on Saturday, *if* he doesn't *kill* us first." Then she looked at JeeBee with an innocent smile. "Are you coming?"

Janet just wouldn't let it go, Theo thought. For the past few weeks, JeeBee had been riding the bus an hour in to Washington, D.C., every Saturday, to get her hair done. When Janet had asked why, JeeBee had answered, "Oh, uh . . . just for fun."

But Janet wasn't buying it. "Why would she go all the way to D.C.?" Janet had said to Theo last week.

"I don't know." He didn't understand what the big deal with hair was, anyway. No matter how long Janet spent in the bathroom, her hair always looked the same.

"But she used to get it done here," Janet said. Then she put her hands to her head. "Of course, the beauty parlor here *is* full of *nitwits*." She still blamed them for not being able to fix the at-home highlights kit she'd tried on herself last summer. The box had said it would make her hair "sun-kissed," but by the time Janet rinsed it out, the look was closer to "blow-torched." The local beauty parlor had to cut most of her hair off, which made her look "like a *boy*!" She'd never forgiven them. Even after a year of egg-yolk soaks, her hair was barely to her shoulders.

"What time does your track meet start?" JeeBee asked.

"Ten." Janet smiled again.

"I'm getting my hair done in the morning, but I'll come watch after lunch."

"Um-hmmm." Janet raised her eyebrows at Theo.

"Those meets do last for hours," Mom said.

Theo agreed. He and Kenny usually stopped by, mostly to bum money from his mom for the snack bar. But to watch the whole thing, you'd be there all day.

"I'm sure Janet will appreciate any time you can spend there." Mom stared pointedly at Janet. Then she turned to Theo. "How was your day?"

"Good. Hey, can I borrow the tape recorder?" He told them about the project. Janet yawned loudly, but his mom, and especially JeeBee, looked interested. He could tell that JeeBee was already thinking of what she would choose if she were in sixth grade.

"How are the kids who don't own a tape recorder doing it?" Mom asked.

"Mr. Meyer said they could bring something in to school and record it on his. But I might want to tape something outside."

"Who knows where this project will take you," JeeBee said.

"Well . . ." Mom thought a moment. "Okay. Just don't let it get wet. Don't drop it —"

"Or let Kenneth step on it." Janet liked to tease Kenny about his big feet.

"Don't let an avalanche bury it," JeeBee added, winking.

"Most importantly," Janet said, "once you stick it under a tree to capture nature sounds, don't pee on it!"

Mom and JeeBee both put down their forks. "Janet!"

After dinner, Mom tidied up the kitchen. Theo followed JeeBee through the living room, stepping around Janet sprawled on the floor in front of the TV. When JeeBee opened the front door, Theo stepped out behind her onto the porch, his stomach fluttering, and closed the door behind them. "JeeBee? You know that card?"

She put her hand on Theo's arm. "I didn't want you thinking he'd forget your birthday."

"How come you signed it this time, and not before?"

"You're getting older. I thought you might be ready to talk about him. If you want."

Theo nodded. He looked down the row of houses. There was probably a dad in each living room, helping his kids do their homework, maybe reading them a story. "What happened to him?"

"I'm so sorry, Theo. I know that's the big question you really want an answer to, and no one can give one."

"I don't know what else to ask."

She squeezed his arm. "It must be so hard — you were only five when he left."

"I don't remember that day at all," Theo blurted out. "I try to, but I can't."

"Well, we had breakfast together. Then your dad gave you and Janet a hug and said he was going to Vietnam to fight for our country. He said he loved you very much and he'd be home soon. Then you and Janet helped me wash the dishes, and your mom took him to the airport."

Theo shook his head. "It's all a big blank."

"Come by my house tomorrow. I'll be home at five. We can talk some more." She patted his arm.

Theo turned toward the house, but then stopped and looked back at JeeBee. "What did we eat?"

"Hmm?"

"For breakfast that morning."

She smiled. "Your dad made pancakes, with smiley faces out of blueberries."

"Oh," Theo said. "The good kind of dad." But knowing this only made him feel worse.

JeeBee moved toward him and pulled him into a hug. "I can help you remember, Theo."

He nodded.

"Good night, sweetheart." JeeBee stepped off the porch and headed home.

Theo opened the front door. Inside, Janet still lay on the floor, the TV blaring. But Mom wasn't watching. She stood in front of her knickknack shelf, lost in thought, looking at The Ladies.

The Ladies were porcelain dolls in long, fancy dresses with gilt edges. Each doll was about eight inches high. Their skin was milky white, their lips pink bows. When Theo was younger, he'd been fascinated with them. They seemed frozen in time, terribly fragile. Years ago, Mom told him and Janet how their dad had given her the first doll on the one-year anniversary of their first date and then another doll on each anniversary that followed. According to Mom, that was way more romantic than giving a present on a wedding anniversary.

That was why the dolls were so important to Mom. He and Janet had grown up hearing her say they weren't to play with, they were only to look at.

Janet had a different name for the collection: The Shrine.

Once when Janet was nine, Mom was in her room with the door closed, lying down with a headache. It was the summer that Dad was supposed to come home, but didn't, and Mom got headaches all the time. Janet and Theo had been tiptoeing around all day, and Janet decided to have a really quiet tea party with The Ladies.

Theo watched from the couch as she carefully took them down from the shelf and set them on the floor in a semicircle. She filled a little teapot with water and poured it into tiny cups.

Janet and The Ladies chatted about the fancy ball, wondering if the prince was going to come. And then all of a sudden Mom was shrieking, "I told you not to play with them!" She flew over, clutching each doll with shaking hands as she placed it back on the shelf. Janet tried to explain that she hadn't being *playing* with them; she'd been *serving them tea*. But when she picked one up to put away, Mom said, "Don't touch them!"

Then Theo heard a splintering sound and Janet's gasp. Mom had clipped a doll on the edge of the shelf.

She sat down on the floor. "You have a whole room full of toys! These are all I have left of your dad!"

Janet ran up the stairs, yelling, "*You're* the one who broke her, not me! I was *being careful*!" She slammed the door to her room. Theo inched toward his mom till he could see the doll in her hands. Its dress was cracked. Part of the gold had chipped off. And Mom was crying.

In all the years since then, he'd never seen Janet touch them, and he never went near them.

Theo now climbed the steps to his bedroom and sat down at his desk. The room filled with the sharp scent of glue as he squeezed a line down the edges of *Saturn 5*'s pieces. He fit the rocket together, wiping the glue that beaded out the sides, then laid it gently on his desk.

He studied the diagram for the launch platform: the solid gray base, the tall tower, the red swing arms to hold the rocket upright —

"Bedtime." Mom's voice interrupted his thoughts. She was standing in his doorway in her nightgown and bathrobe. It was only 8:45. But she looked exhausted.

"In a sec. I want to figure out how to make the launchpad."

"It's late."

"Okay, but check this out first."

Mom took a step forward. "Looks good, honey." She turned to leave.

"Come here. I want to show you."

Mom turned, her face pinched and white as she walked toward the desk.

*This is from Dad,* he wanted to say. "This is the launch platform," he said instead. He showed her the diagram . . . *from Dad.* "It's kinda complicated. . . ." He tried to make sense of how all the pieces fit. "But I just finished the rocket part."

He carefully lifted it up to show her. *This is from Dad,* Theo thought again. "This is —" But when he looked up, he saw that Mom's eyes were closed, her lashes moist with tears.

Theo started talking, saying anything to talk over the crying. "The only thing that's bugging me is that the rocket won't be up there with the other ones. It'll be sitting on the launch platform. I wish it could be up there, though." He set the rocket back down.

Mom took a shaky breath and slowly let it out. She kissed the top of his head and told him to brush his teeth. A few seconds later, Theo heard her slippers shuffling down the hall and then her door closing.

Theo brushed his teeth extra long to make up for the crying. He put on his pj's, climbed into bed, and turned off the light. But he could still see the rocket on his desk, gleaming ghostly white, lying stalled and utterly earthbound.

## SOMETIMES THE HOUSE FEELS SO

quiet, like we're all holding our breath, saying everything except what we're really thinking.

Saying what you're thinking can be dangerous.

I don't talk as much as Janet and Mom. Mostly I read a lot. Right now I'm reading in my moon atlas about Galileo. He was the first person to point his telescope at the sky and publish what he saw. He discovered that Jupiter has moons. He also published the first drawings of our moon, the mountains and craters.

There's a crater named after him, but it's tiny. You'd think they'd name a huge crater after him, or a whole mountain range. Some guys I've never even heard of have way bigger craters. Galileo got robbed.

But there's another thing named after him: a squiggle called Galileo's Rille. Rilles are dried-up riverbeds, only the rivers were made of lava. Galileo's Rille is in the Ocean of Storms, but it looks really peaceful — like some animal dragged its tail and left a trace in the sand.

Galileo said that Earth wasn't the center of the universe; the sun was. He didn't even invent that idea; he just tried to prove what Copernicus had already said.

But his church got mad, even though it was only an idea. They locked him in his house for the rest of his life, just for saying what he thought.

He'd have been a lot better off if he'd kept his mouth shut.

"**YESTERDAY WE BEGAN OUR**
discussion about the *Voyager* project with a simple question: Who are we?" Mr. Meyer waggled his bushy eyebrows. "And we discovered that the question might not be so simple, after all. . . ." He walked over to the bulletin board with another piece of paper. "Here's another question." He tacked it up: WHERE DO WE LIVE?

Theo hesitated, then raised his hand a little bit. "Earth?"

"And you're the perfect person to answer this, Theo — what is Earth like? How is it different from other planets?"

"Well, the atmosphere keeps the temperature pretty constant . . . and . . . water, of course. That's really important because all life-forms —" He felt a ball of paper smack him just above the ear. Even without looking, he knew who'd thrown it.

"Don't get him started, Mr. Meyer," Kenny wailed. "Or I'll have to listen to him for the rest of the afternoon!"

Mr. Meyer laughed. "Fair enough, though you might want to investigate other forms of persuasion, Kenny, besides whacking your opponent on the head." He turned to the class. "Is that what makes Earth unique: water and a constant temperature?"

"Not really," Rhonda said. "Every planet has a temperature."

"But without a constant temperature, we couldn't exist," Theo explained.

"Aha! So *we're* what makes Earth unique?" Mr. Meyer pressed on. "Human beings?"

Nobody said anything. Theo looked at his classmates, then around the room, his eyes finally resting on the posters above the blackboard. Mr. Meyer had said they were three of his favorite sayings. One showed President Abraham Lincoln's wise, kind face and his quote: "Whatever you are, be a good one." Another was of the scientist Albert Einstein, sticking out his tongue. His quote said: "The important thing is not to stop questioning." The third poster was of Groucho Marx, the wacky comedian with the big cigar. His quote read: "Outside of a dog, a book is man's best friend. Inside of a dog it's too dark to read."

Mr. Meyer examined his sunny yellow tie and scraped off a speck with his thumbnail.

Finally Kenny raised his hand. "What about animals?"

Mr. Meyer smiled. "What about them?"

"People think they're more important than animals." Kenny blushed. "But I think animals are just as important."

"Lots of people agree with you, Kenny." Mr. Meyer walked over to the globe sitting on his desk — not the kind with countries, Theo noticed, but the kind with land features and tiny bumps for mountains. "Many scientists think there's life in space. But you're right, Kenny, that Earth has a huge diversity of life. All these different plants and animals exist — fairly peacefully — in a delicately balanced ecosystem." He spun the globe. "Is that what makes Earth special?"

## VOYAGER 1 *AND* 2 *AREN'T THE FIRST*

probes that will study Jupiter. Pioneer 10 and 11 did, too. They also have a message for space aliens, but it's not a golden record. It's this little plaque, a drawing of a man and a woman, and the man is waving hello.

Only they're completely naked; their whole front sides show. So if the probes are found by any aliens, the guy will just be standing there naked, waving.

I saw the picture in a book I checked out from the library. I did not check the book out to look at the picture — I checked it out to read about the space probes. But the picture is in there, too.

One day in my room, I showed it to Kenny, and he yelled so loud that Janet burst in. She took one look at the picture and started ranting about "space porn." She called me a cretin and Kenny a Neanderthal. Then she laughed at us, and now Kenny stays as far away from Janet as he can.

# THEO ASKED KENNY TO COME

over after school. "My mom said we could use the tape recorder," he said. It wasn't exactly true — technically Theo hadn't asked if Kenny could use it, too. But he figured if he were there when Kenny used it, then that was sort of the same thing.

They polished off half a box of Frosted Flakes and then headed out to Theo's tiny backyard, mostly grass with a scattering of flowers and three little trees. They sat down beneath one and waited — forever, it seemed — until a bird finally landed on the branches above.

Theo raised the microphone and pushed the RECORD button.

"C'mon, squawk, you dumb bird!" Kenny said.

"Quiet! You'll be on the tape!" Theo held the microphone a little higher, careful not to lose his grip.

Nothing happened.

Kenny grasped the lowest branch and gave it a shake. "C'mon, squawk!"

The bird flew away.

"Way to go, Kenny."

"It was a dumb idea, anyway."

"Theodore! Kenneth!" Theo looked up to see Janet's head poking out of his window. "You boys play nicely!"

Theo scrambled to his feet. "Get out of my room!"

Janet just laughed and shut the window.

"Listen," Kenny said, standing up next to Theo. "You need something with action." He shifted into sportscaster voice. "Third and ten. Kilmer's back to pass. The rush is on, but he fires it off to Smith. *He's going all the way . . . touchdown!*" He threw his hands up in the air. *"The Redskins win!!!"*

Theo walked over to the porch and sat down on the sun-bleached wood. "But you're already doing football."

Kenny joined him. "Not anymore. I have a better idea."

"What?"

Kenny lay back, tucked his hands behind his head, closed his eyes, and smiled. "Buster."

"Buster? You're crazy! Buster?!"

Buster was the weirdest dog Theo had ever known. He was just over a foot tall, mostly white, with big meaty shoulders and stubby bowed legs. His face was flattened and wrinkled like he'd chased a speeding car that suddenly braked. Knowing Buster, it was altogether possible.

"He put the *bull* in *bulldog*," Kenny's dad liked to say. "Stubbornest dog alive." Whenever Buster had a bone, Kenny's mom said he looked like an old man smoking a fat cigar.

"Yeah, I figure if anyone can understand Buster, it's an alien."

Theo agreed. Buster snorted. He snuffled. He growled and barked. His sneezes sprayed over two feet. He drooled and wheezed. He snored while he slept. His farts were magnificent. You could hear them across the room.

"C'mon!" Kenny said.

Theo grabbed the tape recorder, and they hurried from his small, crowded neighborhood to the wide streets and big lawns of Kenny's. There was plenty of stuff to tape, Theo thought. The question was *why*. The project was supposed to be the most *important* thing about Earth, not the *weirdest*.

They found Buster lying under the dining table, belly up, asleep. He must have tipped over the laundry basket — again — because he had a pair of Kenny's dad's underwear draped over his face. Buster was snoring, and his stubby legs twitched and pumped furiously. Maybe he was dreaming of chasing Mrs. Ashwell's cat, or that he had knocked over Mr. Symon's trash can and was pawing through the garbage, looking for baloney wrappers.

"Let's tape him snoring," Kenny whispered, crouching down on the floor. "Lift that underwear off his head."

Kenny held the tape recorder mic out toward Buster's face and pushed the RECORD button. Theo got down on his knees. The chairs were in the way, but Theo was afraid if he moved one, Buster would wake up. So he eased himself under a chair and gingerly took hold of the elastic waistband.

With a snort, Buster clamped his jaws down, inches from Theo's fingers.

"Aaaah!" Theo knocked his head on the chair, tipping it over. "Ow!"

Buster growled and trotted off, the underwear still locked in his jaws. Kenny clicked off the tape player. "Let's see where he goes."

They followed Buster into Kenny's room. He dropped the underwear on the rug and then sat on top of it.

"Perfect!" Kenny said. He reached into a desk drawer

and pulled out a little camera. "Here, take pictures of him while I play."

"Play what?" Theo asked, taking the camera. Then he winced. "You're not going to practice, are you? Buster *hates* that."

Kenny grinned. "I know." He walked over to his dresser, where his violin lay, and opened the case with a loud *click.*

Buster's head snapped around, his ears perked.

Kenny sat down on the bed, his big feet splayed in front of him. He turned on the tape recorder and tucked the violin under his chin. Slowly he pulled the bow across the strings. It creaked like a rusty gate.

Buster was up like a shot, pacing back and forth in front of Kenny. Theo snapped pictures.

Kenny made the violin squeal.

Buster whined.

He made it squeak.

Buster growled.

He made it screech.

Buster moaned.

Theo lay flat on the floor, scooching back until he could fit both Buster and Kenny into the same picture.

"And now, his favorite song!" Kenny began to play "Twinkle, Twinkle, Little Star," the violin shrieking out the notes.

Buster parked his wide rump, threw his big square chin in the air, and *how-how-howled.* . . .

. . . *howl*—a-bove-the—*howl*—so-high . . .

. . . *howl*—a-dia-mond—*howl*—the-sky . . .

Buster kept howling even after Kenny finished the song. Kenny waited until the last howl faded, then turned off the tape player and patted Buster's wrinkled head. "Good dog!" he said.

## KENNY WAS THERE THE DAY I FIRST

heard the word MIA. It was the summer before second grade, and we'd met this new kid in the neighborhood. We were over at his house, and his mother said she'd heard Mom was a teacher. Then she said, "What about your dad? What does he do?"

I wasn't sure how to answer, so I said, "He's a soldier, but nobody knows where he is."

She said, "MIA! You poor thing!"

I didn't know what she was talking about. But that night JeeBee was over with Mom and Janet and me. While we ate dinner, I asked, "What's 'MIA'?"

Mom started coughing on her food so hard that she finally had to leave the table. JeeBee looked upset, but then she took my hand and Janet's and said, "It means 'Missing in Action.' It means he didn't come back one day from fighting. You can tell people that's what happened to your dad."

It was easier once I had a name for it. I just said "MIA," and then no one asked any more questions.

## EVER SINCE HE'D GOTTEN HOME

from Kenny's house, Theo had been trying to read the instructions for the *Saturn 5* launchpad.

He couldn't concentrate. It was almost time to go to JeeBee's and talk about his dad. He looked at the launchpad diagram, but he couldn't concentrate on that, either.

Finally the clock showed quarter to five. Theo was glad. He couldn't sit in his room another minute.

Downstairs Janet was flopped in the living room, her leg slung over the arm of the couch, her foot pumping up and down. She was eating a banana and reading a magazine.

"I'm uh . . . just gonna take a walk."

"That's fascinating." Janet turned the page. "I'll alert the evening news."

Suddenly Theo realized that Janet might want to come, too. He stood a moment, watching her. Should he tell her where he was going? Would she get mad he hadn't told her about it last night?

Janet looked up. "I thought you were taking a walk?"

"Yeah. I am." JeeBee hadn't invited her, he realized, just him. Theo bit his lip and walked out the door. He could always tell Janet later.

Theo stepped off the porch and hurried down the street. He knew so little about his dad, nothing almost, just that he had been a crew chief during the war — the mechanic who worked on a helicopter and rode in the back during each flight. But that was it. Theo didn't even know what Vietnam looked like.

Back when he first found out his dad was Missing in Action, Theo thought it must be like being lost. Theo had been lost in the woods once. He'd looked up from the pond where he and Janet had gone to see tadpoles, and she wasn't standing next to him anymore. His heart started hammering, and his legs got scratched as he tore through the woods looking for her. Finally he'd sat down on a rock, crying so hard he got the hiccups, until Janet found him, saying, "I had to *pee*! I *told* you I'd be right back!"

Being lost had felt terrible. The woods his dad was lost in were far from home. Was anyone looking for him?

When Theo had explained to Kenny what "MIA" meant, Kenny came up with the idea that maybe Theo's dad wasn't *missing* in action, maybe he was missing *in action*, like he was a spy or something. Top secret government work. They'd both loved this possibility, and soon they were playing a game called "Theo's Dad." They had to keep the game secret because of the undercover stuff, but that made it even more exciting to play. "Theo's Dad" became almost superhuman, like he could practically see through walls and jump ten feet straight up. Kenny even seemed a little jealous that *his* dad wasn't MIA, too. Mom's Rule Number Two finally began to make sense, then: No one was supposed to talk about his dad, ever, because his dad was a secret agent.

And then one day about a year later, Theo had been over at Kenny's. Theo's mom never watched the news, but Kenny's mom did while she made dinner. The reporter said that the remains of three MIAs had been found. Kenny's mom had turned off the TV really fast and started asking Theo a bunch of questions: Did he like French or Ranch dressing? Did he want a wing or a drumstick? But it was no use; Theo had heard the report. That was the first time he wondered if maybe his dad was dead.

Theo walked up the path in JeeBee's little flowered yard, pushing that thought away. They would have told him. Someone would have already told him if his dad was dead.

He tapped on JeeBee's front door and let himself inside. He found her in the kitchen, drinking tea. She'd put out some cookies and a big glass of milk, and there was a box on the table.

JeeBee gave Theo a hug. "Hi, sweetie."

He sat down. "What's that?"

She pushed the box toward him. "Take a look."

Theo slipped off the lid. A dozen toy cars and trucks in different shapes and sizes were piled inside. Most were made of metal, a few of wood. "I remember these!"

JeeBee nodded. "These were your dad's. He got the first one, that one" — she pointed to a wooden fire truck, painted bright red — "when he was four."

"These were my dad's?" Theo remembered playing with the cars when he was little, when he was over at JeeBee's while Mom was in school learning how to be a teacher. Then over the years, Theo had played with them less and less until JeeBee must have finally put them away. Of course the cars were his dad's. Why had Theo never thought of it before?

He emptied the box, sorting the cars into one group and the trucks into another.

"You and your dad used to play with these cars," JeeBee said.

Theo stopped sorting. "We did?"

"You'd make ramps from stacks of books and then race them."

Theo rolled the fire truck back and forth on the table-top. "I sort of remember. . . ." A hazy memory came back to him of JeeBee's long wooden hallway. "Did we race them down the hall?"

JeeBee laughed. "It was the longest stretch in the house without any furniture to get in the way."

"I remember now." Theo began to line up the cars, big to small.

"Your dad used to do that, when he was little. You're a lot like him, you know."

Theo straightened up the line, feeling his heart beat a little faster. "How else am I like him?"

"Well, let's see. Quiet. And curious. Your dad was always trying to figure things out. How things worked." She shook her head and smiled. "He started working on cars when he was fourteen, even though he wasn't old enough to drive yet. He could fix 'em before he could drive 'em."

Theo smiled. "That's pretty weird." But it was pretty cool, too. He wiped the dust from the top of each car with his thumb.

"Some kids did think he was weird, at first." She laughed. "But then when they got older, they kept bringing their cars by for him to fix!"

Theo laughed, too. He plucked a cookie from the plate and took a big bite. "What else did he do?"

As Theo ate, JeeBee shared stories about his dad: how he built a trellis for her roses, how he saved his allowance to buy comic books, how he once pitched a tent in the backyard and slept there all week, just to see if he could. She spoke of his love of fine craftsmanship and the satisfaction he got from working on an engine until it hummed.

"So smart with his hands," JeeBee mused. "He never thought he was smart enough for your mom. But I told him he was. Just a different kind of smart, that's all." She sipped from her cup. "You're a mix, you know. Book smart like your mom but smart with your hands, too."

Theo drained his milk and set the glass down

carefully. "JeeBee, what did he do in the war? All I know is that he fixed helicopters."

"Theo, look. I want to tell you about your dad. But the war was . . . complicated." She shook her head. "It's hard to explain. I'll tell you what I know about the war. But I think it'll all make more sense if you get to know your dad a little better first. Can you trust me on this?"

Theo shrugged. "I guess."

JeeBee looked at her watch. "It's getting on toward six o'clock. You should probably get home." She stood. "Why don't you come by tomorrow afternoon? I promised to make some cookies for the bake sale at Janet's track meet. You can help me." She kissed Theo on the head. "Gingersnaps. Your dad's favorite."

As JeeBee walked him out, she placed her hand on his back. "Listen, Theo. Your mom and I . . . well, I'm not sure she'd like us talking about this. She thinks if we never talk about your dad it will make it easier that he's gone."

Theo flushed. "What do *you* think?"

"That you're old enough to decide for yourself." JeeBee opened the front door. "So for now, maybe we should keep these talks between us, okay?"

"Okay," he agreed.

And maybe, Theo thought as he walked down JeeBee's flowered path, he should wait a little while to say anything to Janet. She blabbed so much, she might just blab to Mom — and if Mom found out, Theo might never get another chance to learn about his dad. He'd waited so long. He decided to find out all he could and *then* tell Janet, kind of like a report.

As he walked back home, he passed by all the little houses, noticing the cars in people's driveways. His dad could have fixed any one of them when he was only fourteen. His dad was curious — he liked to figure things out. Theo had learned more about him in one afternoon with JeeBee than he had from his mom in his whole life. Why was it so important to his mom to pretend his dad had never existed? And that everything was perfect on the surface?

When he opened the front door and walked into the living room, Janet was watching TV, and Mom was dusting The Ladies with a feather duster.

Mom smiled at him. "Oh, good, you're home. Let me just finish this up, and then we'll eat. I got pizza."

She dusted the broken doll, then tucked it in back, behind the other ones, so that the damage was hidden.

But when Theo looked carefully past the line of perfect dolls, he could still see the crack.

"Mr. Meyer," Cynthia announced the next day, "I've finished my *Voyager* project. Do you want me to bring it in on Monday?"

Theo peered at her as if she were some kind of freak. She was done *already*? They'd only had the assignment *four days*!

"That's a good question." Mr. Meyer walked over to the calendar on the wall. "Let's see. Today's Friday, and the project is due a week from next Wednesday. So that leaves . . ." He counted. ". . . twelve more days."

He turned to the class. "I'm very happy that one student is already done."

Cynthia beamed.

"But let's wait a bit to bring things in. I'd like the rest of you to come to your own conclusions and not be influenced too much by what others choose."

Cynthia scowled.

Theo stifled a laugh.

Mr. Meyer picked up a piece of paper from his desk and walked toward the bulletin board. Theo wondered what question he'd put up next. The paper read: WHAT CAN WE DO?

"You mean, like walk and talk?" Theo asked.

Kenny nodded wisely. "I can walk, talk, *and chew gum, all at the same time.*"

Mr. Meyer smiled. "Very admirable, Kenny." Then he turned to the class. "Tell me something you can do."

Cynthia raised her hand. "I play the flute."

Mr. Meyer nodded. "Good." He wrote it on the board. "What else?"

"I can swim," Joey said. "And I'm learning to high dive."

"Good," Mr. Meyer said, writing that down, too. "What else?"

"I make models," Theo said.

"Nice." Mr. Meyer rolled up his sleeves and loosened his fish tie. Pretty soon the board was covered with skills and tricks like burping on demand, which Kenny demonstrated twice.

"And I bet we could come up with even more," Mr. Meyer said. "We often define ourselves by what we do. I am a science teacher who likes to draw and play tennis." He pointed to Kenny. "And Kenny is a walking, talking, gum chewer. Who burps." Mr. Meyer gestured toward the bulletin board of questions. "So, does *what we do* define *who we are*?"

When the bell rang, Theo saw Kenny walking out with Joey and William. "Hey, where you going?"

Kenny turned around. "Boy Scouts. We're planning our campout." He blushed. "Sorry."

"Right." Theo watched them head toward Room Five, where the Boy Scouts met. Then he walked home by himself.

Two years ago, when Kenny joined up, Theo had gone with him to the first meeting. It sounded like fun: campouts, cookouts, making go-carts. It sounded like a lot of fun.

"Have your dads call me at home," the troop leader had said. "I'd like to get a lot of participation." He'd handed out slips of paper with his phone number. Theo had taken one, crunched it into a ball, and stuffed it in his pocket.

"It doesn't have to be a dad," Kenny'd said later, as they walked home.

But Theo just shook his head. What was he supposed to do, go camping with his mommy? "It sounds dumb, anyway."

Kenny still did Boy Scouts, but he never talked to Theo about it.

Theo dumped his books, grabbed his camera, and jumped on his bike. He wanted to take his *Voyager* picture before he went to JeeBee's. He passed the already-built houses, each one just like the others except for the color of the front door. He rode onto the street with the still-being-built houses and snapped a picture of the workmen nailing up the wooden framing.

There. Done. Now he just needed to figure out the sound part.

But as Theo was riding back through the subdivision, something was bothering him. He passed each house: blue door, brown door, green door — over and over. Every one looked just like every other. The plants in the yards were different. A few had little benches under the front window. But the blue-brown-green houses were all the same.

He slowed to a stop, looking up and down the street, thinking back to science class and all the things Mr. Meyer had written on the board: WHAT CAN WE DO? We can build. But these houses looked like they'd been stamped out of a machine. They seemed so, well, *ordinary*. He didn't want to choose something ordinary for his assignment.

He pedaled on toward JeeBee's neighborhood. Who did he know who could do something extraordinary? And then it hit him. His dad. His dad could fix a whole car when he was only fourteen. Theo didn't know a single other kid who could do that.

Theo felt a surge of pride. He pedaled harder, his legs strong. When he passed by the woods at the edge of town, he detoured toward them. There was a dirt trail he liked to ride on, through the trees. He pumped harder, picking up speed.

Near the bottom of the hill was a dirt mound, a couple feet high. He and Kenny had experimented — if you were going fast enough and pulled up on your handlebars just as you hit the mound, your bike flew off the ground. You had to be careful, because there was a big stump sticking up and when you landed, you had to brake and steer *fast* out of the way.

Theo pumped down the hill, his camera swinging back and forth on its wrist strap, his thigh muscles burning. Harder . . . harder . . . *pull! He was up! He was flying!*

He landed with a thud, braking hard, veering quickly to avoid the stump. WHAT CAN WE DO? Well, Theo could *fly!*

What about a picture of him flying on his bicycle? Would that be a good thing for his *Voyager* project? Theo didn't know what he wanted to choose.

All he knew was he wanted it to be special.

He pulled up to JeeBee's front lawn and dumped his bike on the grass, careful not to crush any flowers. Then he tapped on the door and let himself in. He found JeeBee in her kitchen. She gave him a hug. "Hi, sweetie. Did you already have your snack, or do you want to wait for the cookies?"

"I'll wait."

"The dough is made," JeeBee said. "Let's get rolling." Theo washed his hands, then helped JeeBee form the dough into small balls, which they rolled on a plate of sugar. They placed them on a cookie sheet in little rows. "Your dad could eat a dozen cookies in one sitting. He used to pop them into his mouth whole."

"Did he ride his bike a lot?" Theo asked.

"Not as much as you do . . ." JeeBee slid the first pan into the oven. "But he had to ride his bike to the auto parts store whenever he had his engine pulled apart."

Theo tried to imagine his dad as a kid, riding his bike. "Did he and his friends ride together?"

JeeBee shrugged. "Mostly, your dad was a home-body. He really was happiest just puttering out in the garage." She scraped down the mixing bowl. "Your mom was good for him that way. She made him get out of the house and socialize."

"*Mom* did?"

JeeBee sprinkled more sugar on the plate. "Yes."

"Was she different then? 'Cause now she works and does stuff at home, but she doesn't go out with friends that much. And she goes to bed so early."

JeeBee put her sugary hand on top of Theo's. "I think she's pretty tired from work and raising two kids. But she loves you very much."

Of course, Theo knew this, but it felt good to hear, anyway.

As they rolled more dough balls, JeeBee said softly, "You can imagine how scary it was for your mom to be raising you and Janet while your dad was at war, and then find out one day that he was missing. She's done remark-ably well, considering all she's been through."

Theo knew it had been a lot of work for Mom, raising him and Janet. But it had never occurred to him that it would be scary, too.

The kitchen filled with the sweet, spicy scent of cookies baking. "You must be starving," JeeBee said. "Why don't you get a glass of milk. The first pan is ready." She pulled the cookies from the oven and put some on a plate. "You know, your dad used to help me make cookies, when he was little. I think it reminded him of playing with clay. In fact, he told me he *ate* a ball of clay once, as an experiment to see if it would taste good."

Theo grabbed a cookie and bit into it even though it was still hot.

"Your dad never could wait, either. He was always hungry." She put more balls of dough on the cookie sheet. "Hated army food, though. *That* was hard on him."

Theo took a long drink of milk to cool his mouth. "How do you know that?" But then he figured it out as soon as he asked. Of course. "He wrote you letters."

The smile faded from JeeBee's lips.

Theo thought back to the war movies he'd seen, all set during World War II. In his mind's eye, he saw long rows of soldiers marching like they were in a parade, enlisted men springing to attention, saluting when an officer entered the barracks, tanks rolling over snowy fields, and then the soldiers marching, marching again. When had his dad had time to write?

"Can I see his letters?" Theo said.

"Theo . . . I thought we decided you were going to get to know him first."

"But reading the letters will help me do that."

JeeBee wouldn't look at him. "I thought we were going to wait. . . ." She put the cookie sheet in the oven.

"I've *been* waiting. For five years."

"Theo, you need to understand. Sometimes in war people are asked to do things that they wouldn't usually do." JeeBee looked at him now. "You might not like everything you read."

"I don't care."

JeeBee thought for a moment and then walked over to the dining room cupboard and opened a drawer. She came back with a small bundle. "This is something else you might want to keep just between us. For now." She handed him the stack of letters.

Theo pulled out the top one, sat down, and opened it.

> Hey Ma,
>
> I'm here. Long flight! Sure miss your cook-
> ing — army food stinks!

*I don't want you worrying about me any. All I
have to do is keep my helicopter running smoothly.
The <u>other</u> guys do all the tough stuff.*

*Some of the guys just stopped by. I was
telling them about you. I mentioned how good
your cookies are and they all said to say a big
"hi" for them.*

*Love,*
*Vince*

*P.S. Just kidding. You don't really have to send
cookies.*
*P.P.S. If you do send some, better not do
chocolate chip — I think they'd melt.*
*Gingersnaps would hold up pretty well, though.*

JeeBee read over his shoulder. "I sent cookies, every
month. I don't know how often he got them, but I sent
them." Her lower lip started trembling. "In case he
got hungry between meals." She dabbed her eyes with a
tissue. "I didn't know what else I could do."

A fuzzy memory came back to Theo of packing cookies in a box. He must have been five. "I remember," he
said. "I helped you."

JeeBee patted his shoulder. "Take the letters home, if you like, and we'll talk some more after you've read them."

"Thank you, JeeBee."

As Theo hurried out to his bike, he stuck the letters under his shirt and then tucked it in. He pedaled home so hard he was sweating by the time he reached his house. Mom was still at work, and Janet at practice. For once Theo was grateful for the quiet. He ran up to his room, his hands shaking as he pulled out the letters. Then he remembered what JeeBee had said and closed his door.

Ma,

I'm missing that nice Virginia springtime. They don't really have spring here. They just have two seasons — wet and dry. The rains are supposed to start in May. Hope that cools things down. It's been close to 100 all week. In the shade it's okay, if there's a breeze and you don't have to move.

Forget the cookies — send ice cubes!

Kiss Theo and Janet for me.

Love,
Vince

"Kiss Theo and Janet. . . ." So Dad must have loved him. Theo had always believed it, but still, here was proof. He opened the next letter.

Ma,

Don't worry! I'm sorry I haven't written in a while. I'm fine, just really busy.

You asked what a typical day is for me over here. Every day I get up early and check over the helicopter. I get her ready to fly. The pilot likes to look things over, and I want to make sure she's ready when he comes out. Then we go get breakfast. Sometimes we talk about where we're going to be flying, but sometimes we just talk about baseball. Don is a Yankees fan but a nice guy anyway.

When we're in the air, I sit in the back of the helicopter. I tell Don about any ground conditions like tree stumps at the landing zone that might make it tricky for us to land or take off.

The gunner and I keep an eye on things while the guys we're transporting unload, then we head home. I look over the chopper after each

flight, and do a longer inspection at the end of
the day. I like to keep her clean, and that can
take a while.

Oh yeah, and there's time for eating the
army's version of food — that's a _real_ treat.

So as you can see, there's no need to worry
about me. My biggest danger is a case of indi-
gestion from the great chow here. . . .

Dad sure talked about food a lot. And he was still
always hungry, even though he was a grown-up. That
was something he and Theo had in common.

. . . Kiss the kids.

Love,
Vince

P.S. Theo's birthday is coming up. Could you
pick out something for him? He seemed to
like that model plane we built last year —
something like that?

So that's how the models started, Theo realized.
JeeBee must have said the first time that it was from Dad,

though Theo didn't remember this. And after that, everybody just knew, like it was a family tradition. But what struck Theo the most was that Dad had remembered his birthday, even in the middle of a war.

He opened the next letter.

> *Dear Ma,*
>
> *Well, of course we have a gunner on our helicopter, Ma. I have a machine gun, too, but I don't have to use it much. . . .*

Wait a minute. A gun? Dad was a mechanic! Why would he need a gun?

Did that mean he shot people? Theo flushed, the skin prickling on his face. Was there some kid in Vietnam who didn't have a dad anymore because of *his* dad?

> *. . . I'm sorry if I upset you. You need to not worry about me so much, okay? Mostly, it's pretty routine. Like tinkering on my car like I used to every afternoon in high school. . . .*

Theo heard a tap and his door opening. "Theo?"
He grabbed the edge of his blanket and threw it over

the letters just as Mom walked into the room. "Hi, honey. I just wanted to tell you I was home."

Theo's heart hammered so loud he could barely talk. He gave a little wave from the bed.

"Is everything alright? Why is your door closed?"

"Uh . . . I was just going to change. I spilled my snack."

"Oh. Did you clean it up?"

"Yep." Theo stood, careful not to uncover the letters, and walked to his dresser. "I'll be down in a minute, Mom."

"Okay." She left the room, closing the door behind her.

Theo raced back to the bed and scooped up the letters. He needed a hiding place. Not his dresser drawers — his mom always put away his clean clothes. Not his desk drawers — Janet snooped. He looked around his room. He pulled some books in his bookcase forward so that he could slide the letters behind them. But first he quickly finished the letter he'd been reading.

*. . . yesterday we had a beautiful flight at sunset over a field of green rice paddies. It*

*was so peaceful, I almost forgot why we're here.*
*I wish you could have seen it.*

*Love,*
*Vince*

*P.S. I'm growing a mustache, did Rosemary*
*tell you? I wrote her about it.*

The line hit him square in the gut. Rosemary was his mom. If Dad wrote to her, too, did that mean that somewhere in his house there might be a whole other stack of letters?

The next morning Theo sat in the living room, turning the pages of the photo album. He knew he wouldn't find what he was looking for — he already knew what was on every page. But he looked anyway.

"You sure were an ugly baby." Janet walked by in her warm-up suit and turned on the TV. She liked to watch Saturday morning cartoons while she stretched for her track meets. She leaned forward from the waist until the palms of her hands touched the floor. "Are you coming to watch me run?"

"Maybe after Kenny's," Theo said. "I promised I'd come over and help him this morning."

"It's my last meet." She sat down on the floor, stuck one leg out straight, and bent the other one behind her. "Besides, I need you to watch and see what time JeeBee gets there." She lay back, groaning softly. "I was thinking, maybe JeeBee's getting her hair fixed at a fancy shop in D.C. 'cause she wants a boyfriend."

"A boyfriend?" Theo said. "But she's sixty."

Janet sat up. "Sixty isn't that old. Besides," she went on, sounding like one of her magazines, "mature women can still be attractive."

Theo flipped through the photo album to pictures of three-year-old Janet in a pointy birthday hat, with frosting on her cheek, and baby Theo sitting on Mom's lap, reaching for the cake. "But it's JeeBee."

Janet switched legs and lay back down, groaning again. "Okay. Maybe she wants a job."

"As a hairdresser?"

"No, you nitwit. Maybe she wants to look extra nice so she can *get* a job."

Theo turned the page to see Janet, riding a pink tricycle. "But she has enough money."

"That's not the only reason to work, Theodore."

He flipped the pages again to see himself, riding the same tricycle while Janet zoomed past on a new purple bike with training wheels. He couldn't believe his parents made him ride a pink trike. "Why would she want a job if she didn't need money?"

Janet sat up again and stretched her legs out straight. "Self-fulfillment. She never got to work when she was young. Maybe she wants to reach her full potential."

"But she's *sixty*."

Janet reached down and grabbed her toes. "Mature women can bring a lot to the workplace."

Theo shrugged. "Maybe." On the next page, he knew, were pictures of Dad, barbecuing in the backyard.

Mom walked past, holding a basket of laundry. "Looking at baby pictures?"

He took a deep breath and tried to make his voice casual. "I was looking for Dad."

He saw his mom stiffen. She didn't turn around.

Janet sat up, her eyes big.

Mom put the laundry on the table. When she turned around, she had a smile pasted on her face, but her eyes looked scared. "He's in there." She found the picture of him, standing by a grill. "There. There's your dad."

"Not these; I've seen these before." Was it true what

JeeBee said — that Theo was old enough to decide for himself? If JeeBee could disagree with Mom, maybe Theo could, too. "I want to see a picture of him in Vietnam."

Janet's eyes were humongous. She got up and stood behind Mom, shaking her head.

Theo ignored her. "Did he write to us?"

Mom stared like she didn't understand what he'd said. Janet was making the "cut" sign across her throat.

"Do we have any letters from him?" Theo asked again.

Suddenly it was like his mom woke up. "No. We don't." She wheeled around, almost bumping into Janet, and snatched up the laundry. "We're leaving for your track meet in half an hour, Janet." Then she hurried from the room.

"What are you, crazy?" Janet hissed as soon as Mom was out of sight. "You know she hates to talk about him!"

Theo flipped through the rest of the album. "I just wondered if there were any letters."

"Why do you care?" Janet's cheeks grew red. "*He* doesn't."

Theo thought of Dad's "Kiss the kids" at the end of all his letters. "How do you know?"

Janet launched forward until her face was about two inches from Theo's. He could feel her breath on his skin. *"If he cared about us, he'd be here."*

"But he can't be here. He's MIA."

*"Just forget about him, Theo!"*

There was a tap at the front door and JeeBee walked in, humming.

Janet bolted upright. She looked at JeeBee and burst into tears.

"Oh my goodness! What's wrong?" JeeBee rushed over to her.

Theo opened his mouth.

"Don't," Janet warned him through her tears.

JeeBee put her arms around Janet and patted her back. "What happened?"

"Um . . ." Theo stalled. Janet glared at him. Then he had it. "Greg Brady. She just heard he's getting married."

"Who's Greg Brady?" JeeBee asked.

"He's on *The Brady Bunch*," Theo said.

"Oh, for heaven sakes, Janet." JeeBee's voice was calm and comforting. "You shouldn't cry over a television actor. He isn't who he plays on TV. In real life, he's . . . he's probably self-absorbed and conceited."

"Yeah," Theo added, "maybe his feet smell."

"Greg Brady's feet don't smell!" Janet said, still crying, but she was smiling now, too.

JeeBee put her hands on Janet's shoulders. "Now dry your tears. No use crying over a TV star. Somewhere out there is a young man who's perfect for you."

"Frankenstein," Theo suggested.

Janet laughed and, for once, didn't throw anything at him.

"Now I need to hurry if I'm going to catch my bus." JeeBee let go of Janet. She set her big white purse down on the coffee table and opened it. "But I thought I'd drop these off."

"Cool!" Janet said, looking into the purse, but then she frowned as JeeBee pulled out an envelope.

"Pictures of your birthday. I made extras for you." She handed them to Theo, tucked the rest back in her purse, and snapped it closed. "Thank you for making the pictures extra special, dear," she said to Janet.

But Janet didn't answer. She was staring at the purse.

Theo looked at the first photo: his thin face and brown hair, a worried look in his eyes. In all the photos, he discovered, Janet had made bunny ears behind his head with her fingers. "Thanks a lot, Janet."

"Huh? Lemme see." She came around to look over his shoulder, pointing at the one of Theo blowing out the candles. "Is that a booger?"

"A lovely thought, dear." JeeBee headed for the door. "I'm sure I'll think about it all the way downtown." She shut the door behind her.

Janet pounced on Theo. "See, I *told* you something's going on! I saw *inside* her purse. . . ." She paused for effect. *"Gumballs."*

"Gumballs?"

Janet nodded slowly. "A whole bag of bubble-gum balls."

"So what?"

"Theo!" Janet grabbed his arm and gave it a shake. *"Get real!* JeeBee's *sixty* — she doesn't chew bubblegum!"

"Well, why didn't you ask her about it, if it's such a big deal?"

Janet huffed. "I didn't want to *tip her off.* It's a *clue:* She's *up* to something. . . ."

Theo looked out the window and saw JeeBee turning the corner. "Like what?"

"I don't know." Janet wiped her nose on her sleeve. "But I'm going to find out."

● ● ●

After Janet and Mom left for the track meet, Theo stood outside Mom's room, his heart racing. He knew he wouldn't get caught, but he'd never snooped through his mom's stuff before.

He walked in and surveyed the room. Where would his mom keep a bunch of old letters? By her bed? He walked over to her nightstand. A delicate gold alarm clock and a lamp with a stained-glass shade sat on top. He took a deep breath and pulled open the little drawer.

Candy wrappers?

Five . . . no six, candy-bar wrappers!

There was also a book. The cover had a fancy lady in the arms of a muscled man. She looked sort of like the porcelain dolls downstairs, only her dress was way tighter and curvier than anything The Ladies wore. A romance novel, Theo thought. That's what it was called.

Had Mom laid in bed, reading and eating six candy bars? She'd never let Theo or Janet do that. He shut the drawer and walked over to the big dresser against the wall. Maybe the letters were in there.

The top drawer was a jumble of socks and undies — Theo took one look at his mom's bras and shut the drawer, fast. The middle drawer held T-shirts and jeans. He shut that and opened the bottom drawer.

Theo couldn't believe it! A huge mess of books — more fancy ladies in tight dresses and big musclemen — mixed up with a treasure trove of sweets. Candy bars. Marshmallow cookies. Licorice sticks. A bag of caramels. It was like Halloween without the duds, just the good stuff. A whole drawer full!

Was this what Mom did when she went to her room and shut the door — ate candy and read about romance? Theo thought she was in her room crying or lying down with a headache!

He grabbed a marshmallow cookie from the package and stuffed it into his mouth as he looked at the book covers. He ate another cookie, and another. Then he grabbed two candy bars and pushed the drawer closed. Theo looked around the room, working cookie out from between his teeth with his tongue.

There was a nightstand on the other side of the bed — Dad's nightstand. The top was empty, but there was a drawer. Theo crossed the room and opened it.

The drawer held just one thing, a small sketchbook. Theo flipped it open. On the first page was a drawing of a convertible, low and lean with huge fins in back. The driver had dark hair and sunglasses. Dad? The picture was signed *Vince Perry '61*. Dad had drawn it back in high school.

Theo sat down on the bed, unwrapped a candy bar, and looked through the sketchbook. There were more cars, all souped up, some with bursts of flame shooting out the exhaust pipe and the too-cool guy behind the wheel. And the pictures were *good*, Theo thought, biting into the chocolate bar. No one had ever told Theo that Dad could draw.

He flipped the page: *Rosemary's Roadster*, the picture was titled. It was another convertible with big whitewall tires, but now there was a teenage girl at the wheel. Mom? The next page: *Rosemary's Race Car*. Mom looked so young, so cool. Theo never thought about his mom as a teenager. A final page: *Rosie the Rebel!!!* In this one Mom was driving, a wicked grin on her face, her hair flying back as the car sped forward.

The mom Theo knew now drove the speed limit. In a station wagon. What had happened to his mom the rebel?

Dad's drawings looked like they were made by a funny kid, one who was usually quiet but every once in a while said something that made the whole class laugh.

Theo replaced the sketchbook and shoved the rest of the candy bar into his mouth. There was only one place left to look for the letters: the closet.

His mom had taken over all the space, Theo discovered. Had she thrown away Dad's stuff? But then Theo noticed the stack of boxes, shoved to the side. Theo opened one. Inside were Dad's shirts, folded haphazardly, a wool jacket on top. It smelled a little stale, but musky, too, in a nice way. Theo held the jacket to his face and remembered the warm, wet smell of damp wool, of a day when he and Dad had been walking somewhere in the rain and Dad scooped him up and tucked him under his jacket to stay dry.

Theo wanted these clothes. He tried on a blue T-shirt, soft with age. The sleeves hung down to his elbows, but he didn't care. He wanted to wear it anyway. Except if he did, Mom would know he'd been snooping in her room. He put the shirt back in the box.

He pulled out the other boxes. Pants, shoes — Theo couldn't believe how big Dad's feet were. The next box was full of papers. Theo rifled through them, but they were all boring. Insurance stuff. Legal stuff. He ate the other candy bar while he looked.

Finally he found a packet of letters bound by a rubber

band so old it stuck to the paper. The top letter was addressed to his mom:

Rosemary,

Well, I made it. 19 hours on the plane. Look, I know you're still ticked off. You're right, I could have stayed home. But I don't want to keep ignoring my duty to my country just because I have a family. I want Janet and Theo to be proud of me. I'm hoping one day you'll understand that.

Besides, I'm doing this for you, too. By the time I get done here, I'll be able to take a helicopter apart and put it back together again in my sleep! Maybe I'll get a job in aviation, or stay in the service, or — well, we can talk about that when I get home. But a good job that'll pay better than the auto body shop. It will all work out — you'll see.

You're probably wondering what it's like over here. H -O -T. Lots of barbed wire and dust. Helicopters flying off and landing. Can't wait until one of those birds is mine!

*Well, I'm going to get some chow and then try to get some sleep. Don't worry, I'll be just fine.*

*Love,*
*Vince*

*P.S. Kiss the kids!*

Theo had asked Mom if there were any letters from Vietnam, and she'd said no. Had she forgotten about the box in the closet? Theo wanted to think so, but he knew the truth: Mom was lying to him.

But why?

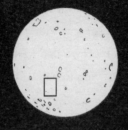

RUPES MERCATOR

# MERCATOR'S FAULT

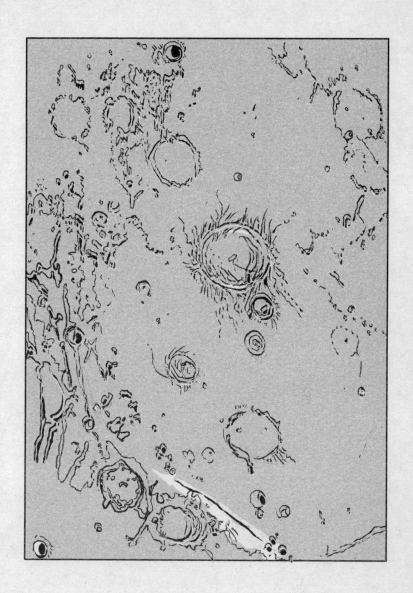

**HAVE YOU EVER BEEN SUCKER**
punched? Punched in the guts when you weren't looking?

Getting punched doesn't feel good, but what really hurts is being suckered.

## THEO SAT ON HIS BED, HOLDING

the letters. He'd told Kenny he'd come over, right after breakfast, but that was before he knew about the letters. They weren't addressed to him; they were addressed to Mom. But he didn't care. If she could lie, then he could snoop.

He opened the next letter and read.

> Rosemary,
>
> Selfish! Since when is serving your country selfish? You think I'm over here playing army or something? I'm not "abandoning" you and the kids — I'm doing my duty! . . .

Is that what Mom thought, Theo wondered, that she'd been abandoned? Who *was* supposed to come first — your family or your country?

> . . . Besides, I already told you I'm doing this for you guys. We can barely make the house payments as it is. How am I supposed to send

*the kids to college, working as a mechanic?*
*This is my ticket to a better job. . . .*

Theo flushed. His dad went to war so Theo could go
to college? They'd argued about whether Dad should
enlist? What else had they fought about?

> *. . . Listen, I'm sorry. I didn't mean to blow up*
> *at you. But I can't believe you think I'm being*
> *selfish. It's just for a little while, honey. I'll*
> *be home soon and you'll see, everything will be*
> *fine.*
>
> *Besides, you're not all alone. My mom's*
> *helping, isn't she? She told me she'd do*
> *whatever she could. Isn't she watching Theo*
> *while you take your classes? Doesn't she pick*
> *Janet up from school and help out around the*
> *house?*
>
> *You'll see. It'll all work out. Just try not to*
> *be mad anymore, okay?*
>
> *Kiss the kids.*
>
> > *Love,*
> > *Vince*

Theo felt all hot. He hated thinking that Mom and Dad were arguing while Dad was at war.

> Rosemary,
>
> Yeah, okay, if you can swing the payments maybe it would be good to trade in the old car, especially since I'm not there to keep her running. If you get a used one, be sure to have one of the guys at the shop check it out before you buy it. . . .

Theo frowned. It seemed weird that Dad would worry about car payments when he was at war.

He scanned down the letter, past the boring stuff.

> . . . Learning all kinds of new vocabulary. The enemy is "Charlie." Our missions are called "insertions" because we insert a group of guys into the jungle. It's all pretty routine, unless the landing zone is hot. "Hot" means that Charlie is firing as we land. Hot is bad, cold is good.
>
> I can't believe how young some of the guys look. They barely have whiskers. They

look like they should be thinking about their senior prom.

I'm sorry you're lonely, baby. I miss you, too. Just keep reminding yourself this is my ticket to a good job. And I don't want you to worry about me. It's nothing I can't handle.

Tell Janet I'm proud her teacher said she's such a good reader. Tell Theo he's lucky — we never had a hamster in my kindergarten class.

Love,
Vince

Theo flipped to the next letter in the stack. His stomach clenched. It was addressed to him and Janet.

Hey kids,

I hope you're being good for Mommy. I'm counting on you to take care of her while I'm gone.

I saw something today that I thought you'd like to hear about. I went to a different base, and at this base were about a dozen dogs! German shepherds. The soldiers take them out on patrol. The dogs sniff out danger and warn the men.

I watched their handlers working with them. The dogs have to learn certain commands, and the trainers have to learn to read their dogs' signals. Once they can talk to each other, they can work together to keep the other soldiers safe. The trainers really love their dogs. I met Duke and Wolf and Prince — good names for brave dogs!

I hope you guys are doing okay. Do what Mommy says. I put four hugs in here. One is for Mommy and one is for JeeBee. The other two are for you.

Love,

Dad

Theo felt a sharp ache in his chest.

He read the letter again, his anger welling up, bubbling over. It was *his* letter — his and Janet's. Mom had no right to hide it from them.

Theo lay back on his bed. Kenny was waiting for him to bring the tape recorder, but the cookies and candy bars were making him feel sick. He rolled over onto his side.

The moon atlas sat on his nightstand. Theo grabbed it and opened it up to his bookmark at the Sea of Clouds. He saw several craters, but his eyes were drawn to a long, jagged line north of the Marsh of Epidemics and the Lake of Fear: Mercator's Fault. Mercator was a cartographer from the 1500s. The fault was a long line left over from an earthquake. Moonquake, Theo corrected himself.

Theo had learned about Mercator when they studied maps in earth science. Mr. Meyer said that Mercator struggled with the same thing all cartographers struggle with when they want to depict Earth: how to draw something shaped like a ball on a flat piece of paper.

Mercator decided to make a grid with lines running up and down and side to side. He made it to help sailors: The straight lines and right angles made it easier to navigate. "The whole thing was very neat and tidy," Mr. Meyer had said. "But if you looked at the map expecting to see what the world looked like, you'd be wrong."

Mercator had to stretch the countries out to make them line up on the grid. The farther north or south you looked, the more distorted the map was. "It's a good lesson for budding scientists such as yourselves," Mr. Meyer had said. "What seems true is not always true."

Theo understood: Your whole life you could look at the world a certain way. And then one day you suddenly find out that you're absolutely wrong.

Theo closed the book and sat up. He still felt sick, but he didn't want to let Kenny down. He slid the letters next to JeeBee's, behind the books in the bookcase. Then he grabbed the tape player, carried it down to the kitchen, and stuck it in a grocery bag.

But when Theo got out to the garage, instead of heading straight to his bike, he walked over to the workbench. He tried to think back to when he was five, when Dad was still home. What had Dad built with these tools? Had Theo helped?

Dad must have stood right here and Theo must have stood right next to him, so little that he probably couldn't even see the top of the workbench. Had Dad picked him up, helped him hold the hammer? Theo tried to remember, but he couldn't.

He laid down the tape player, reached under the bench, and pulled a block of wood from the rag box. He set it on top of the bench and picked up the hammer. Then he reached for a handful of cold, hard nails and pounded them in, one by one.

Theo pedaled down the street on his bike, one hand on the handlebars, the other wrapped around the grocery bag with the tape player.

He was already late, but when he got to Kenny's street, he didn't turn down it. He wasn't ready to sit in some nice house and pretend everything was okay. Everything wasn't okay, and the more Theo thought about it, the more he wanted to keep riding his bike, farther and farther away.

He passed right by Kenny's street and rode to Town Center, a grassy area with trees and a gazebo. A lot of people had gathered. Theo coasted up to see.

On the sidewalk that ran the perimeter of Town Center, people kneeled on the concrete, making drawings, their hands smeared with chalk. Some appeared to be real artists like you might see in a gallery. Others were just people who liked to draw.

Theo remembered that once a year the Parks Department put on an art festival fund-raiser. He had forgotten it was this weekend.

At the end of the sidewalk, Theo spotted Mr. Meyer. He was on his hands and knees, drawing a science lab. He looked up and smiled. "Morning, Theo." A smudge of purple chalk lined his nose.

"Hey, Mr. Meyer."

Mr. Meyer took a swig from his water bottle and looked around. "Beautiful day."

Theo nodded. It was a beautiful day, with a balmy breeze. How could anyone have problems on a day like this? Theo knew the rule: If you *pretend* everything is fine, then everything *is* fine. Only that's not how it felt.

Mr. Meyer sat back on his heels and studied him. "Something troubling you, Theo?"

He looked so calm and quiet, while Theo himself was ready to explode with questions, all wanting to be asked at once. "Why do things get so mixed up sometimes?"

Mr. Meyer nodded. "That's an excellent question. Life is complicated." He set down his chalk. "Anything specific you'd like to talk about?"

There were so many secrets — Theo didn't know yet which ones were his. "I'm not sure."

"Are you having a problem at school?"

Theo shrugged. "No. School's fine."

"Is everything okay at home?"

Theo didn't answer.

Mr. Meyer studied him for a moment. Then he said, "I want you to know I'm here if you ever need me."

"Thanks." If Theo didn't talk about something else, he knew he'd start crying, right here in Town Center. He looked at Mr. Meyer's drawing: a lab table filled with colorful beakers and a flaming Bunsen burner. "I like your picture."

"Well, it's not much." Mr. Meyer shrugged. "But I like the colors. That's one of the reasons I like art and science — there are so many colors." He looked across the square and laughed. "Speaking of which, look at that face." He pointed to a mom and a toddler, smiling as they walked toward him. The little girl's face and shirt were stained red from the Popsicle she was sucking. "My daughter, Claire. Quite a colorful eater."

Theo's chest tightened. Another happy family. "I gotta go help Kenny with his *Voyager* assignment."

"Oh. What did he choose?"

"His dog," Theo answered, and when he saw Mr. Meyer's grin, added, "He really likes his dog."

"How about you?"

Theo shook his head. "I still don't know."

Mr. Meyer gestured toward the art in the square. "Well, there are a lot of ideas right here. Why don't you take a look?"

Theo nodded and pushed his bike around the square. He saw pictures of cats on a bookcase, frogs riding bicycles, a woman drinking tea, a dragon flying a kite, tigers, boats, flowers, fruit. Theo thought of Mr. Meyer's question: WHAT CAN WE DO?

We can create. That didn't feel ordinary. Should he take a picture of this sidewalk for his *Voyager* project? He watched the artists smooth chalk with their fingers. They were so focused on making something beautiful. Something unique.

Dad would have done this, Theo realized. He would have come to Town Center and drawn a hot rod in chalk — maybe put the whole family in the car, maybe even with Theo at the wheel!

He and Dad would have drawn it together.

When Theo pulled up to Kenny's driveway, Kenny and his dad were playing Horse. "Watch an expert," Kenny's dad said, performing a fadeaway jump shot . . . that missed.

Kenny laughed. "That's H-O. I'm gonna mop the floor

with your shirt." He hooked the ball over his right shoulder, crowing, "Nothin' but net!"

Kenny's dad shook his head. "Hey, Theo. I'm about to get creamed. Care to join me?" He picked up the rolling ball.

"You're late," Kenny said to Theo. "You want H-O, you can join in. I've only got H."

"No, that's alright. I'm not feeling so good right now."

"Are you sick?" Kenny's dad asked.

"Too many candy bars."

Kenny's dad laughed. He executed the same hook shot. The ball sank into the net. "Ohhh — there's life in the old man yet!"

Theo sat down in the grass beside the driveway and set the tape player beside him. Buster idled over and sniffed Theo's shoe. Theo gave him a pat on the head. Then he settled back to watch Kenny's dad get slaughtered.

Theo had known Kenny and his dad forever. They'd biked together, gone to the hardware store, made spaghetti. They'd gone to see the Redskins play — twice — and gotten pizza afterward. Theo had seen Kenny's dad in the early morning, reading the paper with a night's stubble still on his chin. He'd seen him asleep on the recliner in the late afternoon, his mouth hanging open.

Kenny's dad always included Theo in everything they did. He always smiled and seemed happy to see him. But he'd never given Theo that sideways hug he gave Kenny when they watched TV. He never treated Theo like a son.

"I can see your knees knocking, old man." Kenny nailed a slick bank shot from the far side of the driveway and then a layup from the left. "I smell a victory!" He moved in for the kill, his signature shot: a free throw with his back to the net. Theo had watched Kenny practice it about a million times.

The ball swished in. Kenny nodded. "Oh yeah!"

His dad picked up the garden hose and started watering the hedge. "I demand a rematch after lunch."

"You're on," Kenny said. "C'mon, Theo." Then he whistled for Buster.

Theo picked up the tape player and followed them into the house. Kenny grabbed a jar of peanut butter from the cupboard. Moments later, Buster's face was planted in his dog dish, dog tags rattling as he studiously licked the bowl. Theo hoped that Buster snort wasn't getting on the microphone — his mom would kill him.

"Give him some more," Kenny whispered.

Theo felt peanut butter smear across his wrist as he plunged his hand into the jar and scooped up a spoonful. "I can't. His head is in the way." He tried nudging Buster's big, broad head to the side, but it wouldn't budge.

Kenny turned off the tape. "*Poo*-key! *Snack*-ums!" His face turned bright red.

Buster looked up, smacking his tongue against the roof of his mouth, tail wagging.

"What did you say?" Theo asked.

Kenny blushed. "Something my mom does. Quick, stick it in." He turned the tape back on.

Theo scraped the peanut butter against the edge of the bowl, his fingers so goopy he almost lost his grip on the spoon. "Can't we use something a little less sticky?"

"Peanut butter makes him fart," Kenny said.

"*Everything* makes him fart."

"Yeah, but peanut butter makes him fart the loudest."

Buster licked the bowl clean and slurped some water. He looked up, stubby tail wagging, peanut butter embedded in the whiskered wrinkles of his face.

"More?" Theo asked. They'd fed Buster almost half the jar.

"Naw." Kenny turned off the machine. "Don't want to make him sick." He looked at his watch. "I calculate about ten minutes."

Buster waddled down the hall. Kenny and Theo followed him. "He does most of his farting while he sleeps," Kenny said.

"I know. I've spent the night at your house."

Buster wandered into Kenny's room and lay down, his head resting on a pair of Kenny's huge sneakers. Kenny pushed the RECORD button and placed the mic near Buster's rear end. Then he lay down next to Buster and started scratching his ribs. "He likes me to do this while he falls asleep."

Buster rolled onto his back, exposing his white tummy. His little legs stuck up in the air. "Help me scratch," Kenny said. "He's getting sleepy."

Theo sat down and rubbed Buster's ribs. He'd never looked at Buster's tummy this closely before. There wasn't much fur there. The skin was taut, freckled, pink as a baby pig and soft as a rose petal. Buster made a sound, half sigh, half moan, and closed his eyes.

"Does this seem weird to you?" Theo whispered, but Kenny didn't answer. His eyes were closed, too. Kenny and Buster looked so peaceful, lying there together. Theo wondered if they did this a lot.

And then he felt a stab of jealousy dig into his chest. Kenny had everything: A big house. A huge yard. A mom who didn't lie. A dog. A dad. "I gotta get out of here."

Kenny sat up. "But what about the tape?"

"This is stupid, Kenny! How long do we have to sit here, waiting for your stupid dog to fart?"

But before Kenny could even speak, they had their answer.

The peanut butter had done the job.

Theo pedaled away from Kenny's house, holding the tape player in one hand, steering with the other. It wasn't fair. Why did Kenny get everything?

Theo took the corners hard, his eyes filling with tears, almost skidding as he made a right turn toward the woods.

He bounced over the rutted ground down the hill to the trail, pedaling furiously, his whole body jerking. The bike veered back and forth as he tried to steer with one hand. Harder . . . harder . . . he crested the mound, yanked up on the handlebars, feeling the tears spill down his cheeks as his front wheel spun to the right. Theo flew higher than he'd ever flown before.

But he was off balance. He barely had time to straighten his handlebars before he landed with a thud, feeling the wind knocked out of his chest as the bike crashed into the stump.

Suddenly Theo flew again, this time over his handlebars. He held tight to the tape player, thrusting out his other hand to break the fall. His eyes closed as he hit the ground.

Theo groaned, rolling onto his back. Everything hurt. His shoulder throbbed, his hand burned, a rock was digging into his side.

He examined his hand, wincing as pain shot down his arm from his bruised shoulder. A layer of skin was scraped from his palm. Dirt caked the wound.

When Theo sat up, he felt dizzy. He was still holding the grocery bag, but it was ripped, and the tape player was dirty. He pushed the REWIND button, relieved to hear the tape spin. He pushed PLAY and heard the strange

Buster noises. Theo let out a deep breath, then cleaned off the tape player with his shirt.

Slowly Theo stood, the ground spinning a little. He looked around to see if anyone had seen him crash, but the hillside was empty. His bike jutted up against the tree stump. He pulled the bike upright and pushed it up the hill.

But something was wrong. He could hear rubber on metal. He examined the front wheel — it was bent at a weird angle. Great. Just great. His mom was going to kill him. She didn't like it when he did "crazy stunts," and when she saw the damage to his bike, she'd be even madder. She hated wasting money.

He wheeled his bike home as quickly as he could, even though it hurt to move fast. He wanted to get his bike in the garage and himself in the shower before Mom got home.

He was relieved to see that her car was still gone. Janet's track meet must have run late. Theo hid the bike behind Janet's in the garage. He wouldn't tell his mom yet. Maybe he could fix it himself.

Theo limped upstairs and took a quick shower, washing away the dirt, tears, snot, and blood, then put on clean clothes and hobbled downstairs. He needed to get working on his bike before Mom got home, but his body ached to lie down. So he curled up on the couch, cradling his pain to his chest.

"What?!" There were voices. Theo was waking up, and there were voices coming from the kitchen. "I don't believe this!"

Theo was still on the living room couch. The last thing he remembered was being so sore that he lay down. The voices murmured. Theo sat up and strained to hear.

"Rosemary . . ." JeeBee's voice. "That's not fair —"

"Fair!" Mom's voice. She was angry. "Don't talk to me about fair!"

JeeBee said something. Theo leaned forward, but he still couldn't make it out.

And then his mom cried, "It's my decision. I say no!"

Janet came down the stairs, drying her hair on a towel. "There you are, you dodo!" She dropped the wet towel on his head. "You missed my last track meet."

"Shh!"

But the voices in the kitchen stopped.

Janet scooted down on the couch next to him. "What's going on?" she whispered.

Theo shook his head. "I couldn't hear very well. They were arguing about something."

Janet frowned. She let out a deep sigh and then stood. "Listen harder next time, baby brother. That's the only way to learn anything around here." She went back upstairs.

That night Theo lay in bed, feeling the wind gust through his open window. He thought back to the argument. What had Mom and JeeBee been so upset about? He tried to remember what they said — that something wasn't fair.

Light flashed outside the window. Theo heard the distant roar of thunder. A storm was coming, and now he could remember Mom's voice. It almost sounded like she was . . . afraid, Theo realized.

*"It's my decision. I say no!"*

Say no to what?

# THERE WAS THIS TIME WHEN I WAS

little, maybe six. A huge thunderstorm woke me up in the middle of the night. Lightning was cracking so close I thought it would hit the house. You could feel each Boom! like a slap on the chest.

I was scared to get out of bed but scareder to stay by myself, so finally after one really loud BOOM!, I went running out into the hall. I crashed into Janet. She said, "Mom sandwich!" and we ran into Mom's room and climbed into bed with her, one of us on each side. We made a Mom sandwich — me and Janet were the two slices of bread.

Then it almost felt like a party, and Mom even went downstairs to make hot chocolate. I started doing that thing where you count seconds to figure out how far away the lightning is. You know, how you see lightning and you count the seconds: "One chimpanzee, two chimpanzee..." and however many chimpanzees it is when the thunder booms, that's how many miles away the lightning hit.

Only me and Janet got into an argument about whether it was chimpanzee or Mississippi and whether each second meant one mile or five. Then Mom came back upstairs with the three mugs. She sat down at the foot of the bed and said it really didn't matter, the storm was right over us, and why didn't we all just enjoy our hot chocolate.

We looked out the window for a while as the lightning flashed. Then suddenly I thought of something, and I asked, "Is it raining on Dad right now?"

Janet called me a doofus. She said, "It's daytime over there. It's sunny on Dad right now."

I guess I knew that. I mean, I knew how day and night worked, but I hadn't really thought about what it meant. I said, "I was just thinking that if it was raining on him, then it would feel like he was here, too. Like he was in bed with us, too."

Mom said, "It is daytime over there right now." She found my toes through the blanket and gave them a squeeze. "But it could still be raining."

## RIGHT AFTER BREAKFAST THE

next morning, Theo grabbed his camera and headed toward Town Center, alone. He felt sore from yesterday's bike crash and mixed-up about Mom. And he still didn't feel like seeing Kenny.

As he walked, he dodged puddles on the sidewalk. Up ahead was the center. Theo picked up the pace. He decided to check out the whole thing one time and choose the best picture.

But when he crossed the street, he gasped. The rain had washed away the pictures, every single one of them. All that remained were wet smears of color.

Theo groaned. He couldn't take a picture of this. His best idea was ruined! He knew he still had ten days until his assignment was due, but for the first time, Theo wondered if it would be enough. What was he going to do now?

As soon as the library opened at noon, Theo was there, pushing down a small wave of panic. Maybe he should be more like Kenny — just choose something funny. He didn't think that Mr. Meyer would give Kenny a very high grade for taping a Buster fart, but it wasn't about the grade. Theo really wanted to tape the most important thing about Earth.

He just needed to figure out what that was.

He marched over to the reference desk. "Excuse me. Where can I find a bunch of pictures?"

The librarian looked up from her papers. She took off her reading glasses. "Pictures of what?"

Theo shrugged. "Everything."

She nodded. "Well, let's see. The best source for pictures is probably *Life* magazine." She pushed back her chair and stood. "They might not have *everything*, but they come close."

Theo had never spent much time in the magazine section — he always went straight to the science books. "We have issues dating back to 1962. Whatever you're looking for, it's probably here."

At first Theo thought she'd made a mistake, because the shelves were full of huge books. But then he realized that each book contained three months of magazines, bound together. He grabbed a volume and sat down on the floor.

"The 100 Events That Shaped America." Theo flipped

through the pages. The invention of the telephone in 1876. The electric lightbulb in 1879. That might be a good thing to choose for his *Voyager* project: Electricity was important.

Theo stopped turning pages. These were *inventions*. They were important, but were they what was most important about Earth? It shouldn't be a *thing*, he decided. It should be — an *idea*.

But which idea? Maybe if he looked at everything that had happened since he was born, something would jump out at him.

He pulled out the issues for May 1965, the month he was born. There was a story on the "new fad" of skateboards, and another on a wild and crazy new music called rock and roll. Maybe Theo should choose the Beatles for his picture. He could put a minute of their music on the tape.

He pulled down more volumes, flipping through pictures till he saw a spacesuit. The article was called "Man on the Moon," and it was about the first three astronauts who traveled to the moon: Buzz Aldrin, Mike Collins, and Neil Armstrong, the first man to walk on the moon. When Neil Armstrong was a kid, he liked to build model airplanes, the article said. Theo smiled at that. And Armstrong got his pilot's license on his sixteenth birthday. Buzz Aldrin had his own pole vault in his backyard. Cool. When he was a kid, he ate whole boxes of dry Jell-O. Mike Collins liked to grow big rosebushes. He'd done a space walk before, on *Gemini 10*. This time he would pilot the mother ship while Armstrong and Aldrin flew the lunar module down to the surface.

Theo wondered if Collins felt robbed because he got left behind. There's no way Theo would get all the way up there and then not walk on the moon.

He remembered that night, even though he was only four years old. It was one of the few real memories he had of Dad.

"Theo, wake up," Dad had said, picking him up and carrying him into the living room. The TV was on. Dad settled him down on the couch next to Mom and Janet. "Wake up, Jay-bird." He tousled Janet's hair.

Janet mumbled something and kept sleeping, but Theo was waking up.

"You can't miss this, pal." Dad squeezed in so that the whole family could share the same couch. Then he put his arm around Theo's shoulder and gave him a sideways hug. "This is important."

"Amazing," Mom agreed. "Imagine — a man on the moon!"

Theo would never forget watching Neil Armstrong, clumsy in his fat space suit, stepping down the ladder of the lunar module, or hearing his crackly voice: "That's one small step for man, one giant leap for mankind." He and Buzz Aldrin bounded across the barren, gray moonscape: no trees, no life at all, just rock and craters and dust. Theo watched until his eyelids drooped. Then he felt Dad carry him back to bed.

Maybe that's what was most important about Earth: exploring outer space, sending men to the moon. What was cooler than that? Theo flipped ahead till he found the footprint. Deep ridges from the tread of Armstrong's shoe, dug into moon dust. He'd read that the footprints were still there. There wasn't any wind on the moon, so nothing had blown them away.

Armstrong and Aldrin spent over two hours walking around. They did experiments to check for rare gases. They set up a meter to monitor moonquakes. They picked up samples of rock and moon dust to bring back to Earth. Before they left, they planted the American flag. The librarian was right: There were pictures of everything here.

Wait a minute. Pictures of everything?

Theo pulled down more volumes and riffled through the pages. . . .

And then he saw them.

A page of little faces, the pictures all lined up in rows like a school yearbook. Maybe two dozen guys, staring right at him. Most were in uniform, clean-cut, looking so brave and serious. "One Week's Dead," the headline said.

The eleven pages that followed showed all the Americans who had died in the Vietnam War in one week. Two hundred and forty-two guys. Theo flushed, his face feeling prickly. All these guys were dead?

He flipped faster now, magazine after magazine. 1967, 1968. He saw men slogging through thigh-high, muddy water, holding rifles. Paratroopers jumping out of airplanes. Men in riverboats, cruising down the Mekong Delta. Everything looked so green — green plants, green uniforms — and brown. So much mud.

Theo knew a little about the war, how even with American help, South Vietnam had lost to North Vietnam. But no one had ever told him there were magazines filled with pictures of the war.

He couldn't believe how many soldiers there were.

They didn't all look sad and scared. Sometimes a group of men posed, looking proud, like they were a team who had just won a football game. Sometimes they even looked like they were having fun.

And suddenly, Theo realized . . . maybe, if he looked through all the pictures . . . maybe, if he didn't get caught. . . .

Maybe, if he wanted it badly enough, he'd find a picture of Dad.

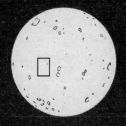

MARE COGNITUM

# KNOWN SEA

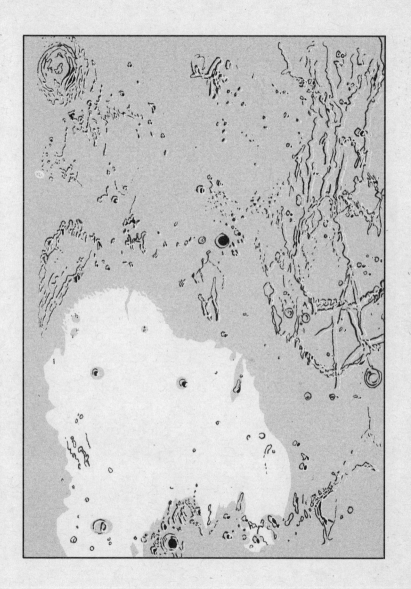

**"DID ANYONE FINISH THEIR**
project over the weekend?" Mr. Meyer asked on Monday.

Theo's stomach clenched. Nine days left. He looked to see who raised their hands: Joey, Sharon, and Elizabeth. Three more kids were done.

"Good." Mr. Meyer smiled. "For the rest of you, here's something else to think about." He put another sign on the bulletin board: WHAT MAKES US HUMAN? "Good, bad — the whole, messy package."

Cynthia's hand shot up. "Love. That's what separates man from beast."

"How do you know that?" Rhonda asked. "You don't think a mama bear loves her cubs?"

"My dog loves steak," Kenny added, shooting Theo a grin.

But Theo didn't smile back.

Mr. Meyer stroked his checkered tie. "Well, let's think about basic emotions like fear, anger, happiness. Do animals feel those things?"

"Buster is happy when I get home from school," Kenny said. "He wags his tail."

Kenny doesn't have a care in the world, Theo thought, slumping down in his seat.

"Ever seen a bunny freeze, trying to hide?" Rhonda added. "That's fear."

"How about anger?" Mr. Meyer asked.

"Isn't that why a mama bear charges to protect her cubs," Rhonda said, "because she's angry?"

"Perhaps. Unless she's charging because she's afraid. Sometimes it's hard to tell those two apart." Mr. Meyer smoothed down his mustache. "How about more complex emotions, say . . . jealousy, or greed, or guilt? Is that what makes us human?"

Theo looked over at Kenny, who was busy trying to balance his pencil on the tip of his finger. He wasn't taking this discussion very seriously, Theo thought, slumping down farther in his seat. Then again, Kenny never took *anything* very seriously, and Theo used to love that about him. Why was it bugging Theo so much now?

He turned to watch Mr. Meyer pace in front of the class. Did he mean what he'd said that day at the chalk festival — that he'd be there if Theo ever wanted to talk?

"Is NASA putting in *all* the bad stuff?" Theo heard himself ask. "Like wars? Stuff like that?"

"Excellent question, Theo. What do you guys think? Should they send up a message of who we really are, or who we'd like to be?"

"I don't think they should put wars in there," Cynthia said. "It's like when you first meet someone, you try to be nice."

Theo sat up. "But we *aren't* nice, not always," he said. "We fight wars all the time."

"That doesn't mean we have to go around blabbing about it," Cynthia countered.

"Yeah," Kenny added. "We wouldn't want to offend our intergalactic neighbors."

"Ah," Mr. Meyer said. "So you think we should be diplomatic?"

"What do you mean?" Theo asked.

"Well, diplomats try to work through difficulties, make things smooth between two countries, and sometimes that involves putting the most positive slant on things."

Theo couldn't help but think of his own family, how always having to pretend that everything was fine felt awful — it felt like lying. "We might only get one chance to make contact. I think we should be honest."

When the bell rang a moment later, Kenny wandered over to Theo's desk. "You wanna come over? We could play football or something."

Theo didn't know if he could stand to spend even one second in Kenny's nice, big, peaceful house. He shook his head. "I can't."

"Oh." Kenny looked uncertain. "What are you doing?"

Theo grabbed his books. "It's private." He caught a glimpse of the hurt and confusion in Kenny's eyes. Then he bolted for the door.

**BEFORE THEY SENT MEN TO THE** moon, NASA wanted to find out what the landing conditions would be like. So they launched a probe to study the surface. They named the area Mare Cognitum — the Known Sea — 'cause it was the first place scientists would really know anything about.

The probe had six cameras mounted at different angles. It sent four thousand pictures to Earth. From far away Mare Cognitum looked smooth. Perfectly smooth. But as the probe came in for a landing, scientists discovered that the surface was actually covered with scars and craters, too small to be detected from Earth.

The closer they got, the more they could see the damage.

## THEO CURLED UP ON HIS BED

with Dad's letters.

*Rosemary,*

*We had a rocky time today. Went to pick up a patrol but the landing zone was hot — - Charlie started firing at us before we'd even touched down. Two of our guys got hit just getting to the chopper. They were wounded pretty bad.*

*When our pilot took off, he made the chopper sway back and forth so that Charlie couldn't hit it. Made me sick to my stomach, if you want the truth, but I didn't complain — just last week one of our choppers was shot down, and those guys aren't writing home anymore.*

*Once we'd cleared out, I thought the worst was over, but then one of the wounded stopped breathing. I had to do CPR the whole way back. Haven't heard yet if he'll make it or not.*

*We drop the guys off in one piece, but they're not always in one piece when we pick them up again.*

*I thought I'd be over here fixing helicopters. I didn't realize I'd be fixing bodies, too.*

*Sometimes the logic of this war escapes me. We keep getting orders to go out on these missions, and our guys are eating it, and it's not even for a good reason. It doesn't make sense.*

*Last week was a good example. We flew a patrol into an area that had been secured months ago, before I got here. Three of our guys had died, helping secure the area last fall. And then we'd abandoned it. So last week we flew more guys in to secure the same place all over again. What was the point of those three guys dying last fall? . . .*

Dad sounded different in this letter. Less confident? More worried? Tired, maybe.

Theo heard the doorknob jiggle. His heart lurched, but then he remembered that he'd locked the door.

"Theodore, let me in!" Janet yelled, pounding on the

door. "What are you doing in there? Are you looking at space porn again?"

"No! Nothing. I'm busy!"

"I hate you!" Janet yelled before stomping off to her own room and slamming the door.

Theo bit his lip. Maybe he *should* tell Janet — it wasn't fair to hide the letters from her. Wasn't that exactly what Theo was mad at Mom for? But if Janet blabbed to Mom, if Mom took the letters away and Theo didn't get to finish reading them, he might never get another chance. Besides, hadn't Janet told Theo to forget about Dad? Maybe she didn't *want* to know more about him.

> *. . . This war is so strange. For days everything is pretty routine: I get the bird ready to fly. We take patrols out and pick them up later. No sign of the enemy. Some days I wonder if I'll ever see them again.*
>
> *Then all of a sudden one day all hell breaks loose and the gunner's firing and I'm firing and trying not to think about how close they're firing back. There's a lot of yelling and then I've got these bloodied kids on the floor of the chopper and somehow I've got to help keep*

them alive long enough to get them to a real doctor.

They really are kids, some of them. Who would have thought at 27 I'd be an old man, but I am. Sometimes that seems to make them feel safer, when they're scared. They look to me for something. I don't know, security. And I try to give it to them, even though deep inside I'm just as scared as they are.

There was this kid yesterday. He'd been wounded bad, and the top of his head was all bandaged, even his eyes. I'm not sure how much of his face was left, to be honest, but his mouth wasn't covered and he was mumbling to me. "Is that you, Ray?" I didn't know if he was going to make it, so I lied. "Yeah, it's Ray," I said.

He got real peaceful then. I held his hand the whole flight in. He was so still and quiet, I had to keep checking to make sure he was breathing.

When we got to base and the medics took over, I let go of his hand. But he got all restless. "Stay with me, Ray."

So I did. I stayed with him, talking really

low and quiet about all the things we were going to do when we got home — how we'd get a convertible and drive down the coast with the top down, stopping whenever we wanted to, doing whatever we wanted.

I never did figure out who Ray was, if it was his brother or his cousin, maybe a friend. But the kid wasn't scared anymore. He wasn't scared when he died.

I heard there's been more protesting against the war. Maybe those protestors are right — I'm starting to think that this whole war was a bad idea. But they are wrong if they think this bad war reflects in any way on the soldiers fighting it. We're just trying to do what our country has asked of us. Anyone who doesn't understand that should spend a day doing what we've been asked to do.

Scoop Janet and Theo up in a big hug and don't let go until I get home.

Vince

Dad sounded terrible. He wasn't just tired. He sounded like he was the one who needed a hug.

In all the other letters, Dad had just sounded like a mechanic, worrying about bolts and levers. But this letter was different. Dad was writing about things he couldn't fix—that no one could fix. Theo wished he could have been there. On that day, Dad had really needed him.

Hi Kids,

Sorry I haven't written very much — I'm pretty busy fixing my helicopter. But I sure like hearing from you. Wow, Janet — you went ice-skating and only fell down once? Great! And Theo — I'm glad you made a new friend named Kenny. It sounds like you two have a lot of fun at recess.

I sure miss you guys. I think about you every morning when I get up and every night when I go to bed and all day in between.

Love,
Dad

Rosemary,

We're heading out. I'll write more later. Just wanted to send you this roll of film. Share

*the pictures with my mom, okay? Tell her not to*
*worry, I'm hanging in there.*

*Vince*


Roll of film? Were there pictures of Dad somewhere?

Theo looked at his clock. It was after five — Mom could be home any minute. But if there were pictures . . .

Quickly, he stuffed the letters behind his books, then peered down the hall. Janet's door was still closed. He raced to Mom's room and looked out her front window — no sign of her car.

He opened her closet. At the very bottom of the box of papers, he found it: a film canister.

Why hadn't she developed the film?

Theo didn't have time to think about it right now. He shoved the box back in the closet, ran to his room, grabbed money from his money can, and ran down to the garage for his bike.

He had to hurry. If Mom saw him leave now, she'd want to know where he was going.

But the wheel! He hadn't fixed it yet. And there was no way he was riding around town on Janet's red bike with silver streamers. That left the old black bike.

The tires were flat. Theo pumped in enough air to get

to the drugstore and hopped on. The seat was high, but he could manage.

He pedaled down the street, a little wobbly, on Dad's bike, now his.

Theo plunked down the roll of film on the drugstore counter.

"Fill out an envelope, kid."

Theo wrote his name, slid in the film, and handed it over.

"These will be back on Thursday." The guy checked over the envelope. "Hey, I need a phone number so I can call you, in case you forget to pick it up."

"You can't call. I won't forget."

The guy shook his head. "Sorry, kid. It happens all the time — people drop off their film and don't come back for it. Then I'm stuck with pictures I don't want and nobody paid."

"I'll pay now."

The guy shrugged. "Sure, whatever. What are these, dirty pictures or something?"

"Nothing like that." Theo handed over the money. "It's a surprise."

● ● ●

Mom's car was still gone when Theo got home. He smelled dinner cooking as he opened the door from the garage. JeeBee was at the stove, Janet at the table, making marks in a magazine with her pen. She was always reading these magazines with quizzes like: IT'S A MATCH: THE PERFECT TARZAN FOR YOU, JANE! and INTIMACY IQ: GET A HANDLE ON YOUR HUNK.

When he walked in, they both looked up at him. Theo flushed.

"Hungry?" JeeBee smiled.

"What's for dinner?"

"Spaghetti."

"Are we having garlic bread?"

"Quiet!" Janet said. "We're busy!"

JeeBee winked at him. "Janet's seeing if I'm a Disco Diva, a Bra Burner, or a Snow Bunny." Then she turned to Janet. "Go ahead, dear. We're on question four, aren't we?"

Theo looked at the magazine article: PERSONALITY PLUS: WHAT YOUR TURN-ONS AND TURN-OFFS SAY ABOUT YOU! "What are you doing?"

Janet huffed in exasperation. Then she said slowly to Theo, like he was an idiot: "Jee-Bee's tak-ing this quiz."

She raised her eyebrows. "So she'll find out her *se-cret* personality. *Get it*, Theodore?"

He didn't, exactly. He didn't know what Janet was talking about half the time, but he thought it might have to do with JeeBee's secret Saturday trips.

"Now that we're done being so *rudely interrupted*," Janet said. "'Number Four: Your idea of a perfect evening is: a) dancing the night away; b) catching the latest exhibit at the local art gallery; c) going to a basketball game.'"

"That's easy," Theo answered. "Basketball."

Janet shot him a stuff-a-sock-in-it smirk. "*You* don't get to answer." And then, "What do you think, JeeBee?"

"Well, I suppose b, going to the art gallery."

"Um-hmmm!" Janet nodded.

Theo sighed and sat down.

"'Number Five: What's your fashion style: a) hot pants and high-heeled boots; b) blue jeans and a sweater; c) a warm-up suit . . .'"

Theo couldn't believe how dumb the quiz was. JeeBee in hot pants? It took Janet over fifteen minutes to finish the questions and tally the results, and then JeeBee's answers didn't really match any of the categories.

Janet pored over the magazine, anyway, making

notations in the margins. Then she said, casually, "JeeBee, can I go downtown with you this Saturday?"

JeeBee stopped stirring the sauce.

"I don't have any more track meets, remember?"

"Oh! Well . . ." JeeBee started stirring again. "Uh . . . *this* Saturday isn't a good time. Maybe some other Saturday."

"Okay." Janet smiled sweetly. Then she grabbed hold of Theo's shirt collar and yanked him out of the room. "See, I *told* you there's something going on. Why *else* wouldn't she want me to come downtown?"

Theo could think of several reasons, but he kept them to himself. "Oh well, I guess we'll never know."

"Yes, we will. I'm going to *follow* her on Saturday." Janet whispered so close Theo felt spit in his ear. "And *you're* coming, too."

Theo headed back into the kitchen. The table was already set, and JeeBee was checking the spaghetti boiling on the stove. He heard the television turn on and Janet laugh at some show. But he stayed in the kitchen to talk to JeeBee.

"Have you been reading the letters?" she asked quietly as she carried the pasta pot over and set it down by the sink.

"Yeah." Theo wanted to tell her about Mom's stash of letters and the roll of film, but something held him back. Would JeeBee get mad if she knew Mom had been hiding things? Hadn't they just been fighting two days ago? Besides, Theo never would have found the letters if he hadn't been snooping. "You know how Dad said he had a gun, but he didn't have to use it very often?"

JeeBee nodded.

"That means he did use it sometimes?"

"Yes."

Theo joined her at the sink. "I always thought he was just a mechanic. I didn't know he shot people."

JeeBee put her hand on Theo's arm. "War is a terrible thing, Theo. It makes good men do bad things —"

Just then the door opened. Mom came in and stopped short. Her eyes darted from Theo to JeeBee and back again. "Is everything okay here?" she asked in a shaky voice.

Theo nodded.

"Why wouldn't it be?" JeeBee pulled a colander from the cupboard and closed the cupboard door with a loud thud.

Mom flinched. "I'm sorry I'm so late. I had a parent conference that ran way over. The parents just kept talking and talking —"

"You're here now." JeeBee clanged the colander into the sink and poured in the pasta to drain. "I made dinner."

"Thanks. It smells delicious. . . ." Mom's voice trailed off.

JeeBee dumped the pasta into a big bowl and ladled on the sauce, but Mom just stood there, holding her purse and a stack of papers.

"You okay, Mom?" Theo said.

JeeBee carried the pasta over to the table and set it down beside a big salad. "Janet!" she called. "Dinner!" Then she dished up the plates.

Theo sat down and put his napkin in his lap. Janet shuffled in and took her seat. But Mom still stood there, hugging her papers to her chest.

"Mom?" he said.

Without a word, she set her things down on the counter and joined them, not even bothering to wash her hands, Theo noted. She and JeeBee both kept their eyes on their plates, forks moving up and down, though neither of them seemed to be enjoying the food.

Janet launched into her latest complaint about her *impossible* English teacher and his *impossibly* long essay assignment. For once, Theo was grateful that Janet talked so much. If Janet weren't doing all the talking, no one would be saying anything at all.

As soon as the meal was over, she planted a big smooch on JeeBee's cheek. "Great dinner. Thanks!"

"You're welcome," JeeBee said as Janet scooted back into the living room.

JeeBee rose and gave Theo a quick kiss on top of the head. "Come by anytime you want to talk, Theo. Good night, Rosemary." She grabbed her purse from the back of her chair.

"Bernadette . . ."

But JeeBee headed for the doorway.

"Thank you for making dinner," Mom said.

JeeBee shrugged. "Kids need to be fed." And then she was gone.

Theo collected the plates to take to the dishwasher. But when he glanced over, he saw Mom still sitting, her hands lying in her lap. "Are you tired?" he asked.

"We're doing okay, aren't we, Theo? You and me and Janet? Aren't we okay?"

Theo straightened up in surprise—he'd never heard Mom express doubts before. Could he have been wrong about her? Maybe she really had forgotten about the letters. Maybe she wasn't a big fat liar after all.

She seemed about six years old, hunched in her chair, looking up at him and waiting to hear his answer.

"Sure, Mom." He nodded. "We're fine."

## THERE WAS THIS TIME WE WENT TO

the airport, when I was seven. JeeBee was coming home from her sister's, and we had to pick her up.

I was real excited to see all the planes. Mom even took us a little early so I could watch them land and take off.

I remember a lot of people there, but I wasn't really paying much attention until some of them started yelling. They had really long hair. At first I thought they were all girls, but then I realized that some of them were boys with long hair.

They surrounded this guy in a uniform. He'd just walked up the ramp from a plane and he was trying to get past them, but they were blocking his way. I saw the uniform and suddenly I was running toward him, saying, "Mom! It's Dad!"

She said, "Wait, Theo!"

I pushed my way through all the people, but when I looked up, it was some guy I'd never seen before.

I backed away but got tangled up in the crowd. I yelled, "Mom!" and then all the people closed in on the guy, saying, "Making another kid cry? Baby killer! How many babies did you kill over there?" And then I started crying 'cause at first I thought maybe the guy would kill me.

Only here's the thing — even though he was this big, strong guy, when I looked up at his face, he didn't seem like he could kill anyone. He looked like he was going to cry, too.

## THEO LINGERED AFTER CLASS,

slowly stacking his books. Kenny headed toward the door with Joey and William, then glanced back over his shoulder at Theo. Theo looked away. He was planning to go to the library, but he wanted to talk to Mr. Meyer first. Alone.

"Have you decided yet what you're doing for your *Voyager* project?" Mr. Meyer asked while he erased the blackboard. "I'm looking forward to seeing what you choose."

"Everything I think of seems dumb."

"You'll figure it out, Theo." He put down the eraser and brushed off his hands. "I have great confidence in you."

Theo looked at the globe on Mr. Meyer's desk — no countries, no boundaries at all, just oceans and rivers and land. "Were you in the war?"

Mr. Meyer's eyebrows shot up. "Vietnam?" He sat down on the edge of his desk. "No. I was in college so I didn't have to go. Some guys from my high school went, though."

"What happened to them?" Theo's throat got tight. "Were they okay?"

Mr. Meyer loosened his sky-blue tie. "Well, they all came home. One lost a leg. Another one has had trouble holding down a job and getting on with his life. But the rest of them are okay. They're working and getting married and raising families."

"Just regular dads."

Mr. Meyer nodded. "Just regular dads."

Theo blinked. Why did he feel whenever he talked to Mr. Meyer like he was going to cry?

"Theo, look. I don't want to pry, but . . . I've heard a little bit about your situation at home . . . from some of the other teachers."

Theo flushed. It had never occurred to him that his teachers might already know. "What have you heard?"

"That your dad never came home from the war. That he's missing."

"We can't even talk about it," Theo blurted out. "Every time I try, my mom just freezes up."

"Do you think it makes her too sad? Or that she's trying to protect you?"

"I don't know." Theo swallowed around the lump in his throat. "What she really wants is for us to forget him."

"Have you told her how that makes you feel?"

Theo shook his head. "When I try to, she looks like she's going to cry, so I stop."

Mr. Meyer thought for a moment. "You're not the one making her sad, Theo. The *situation* is. You can still tell her how you feel."

Theo shook his head. "You don't know my mom. . . ."

"I don't know her well," Mr. Meyer conceded. "But I do know she loves you. Just think about it, okay?"

Theo nodded.

Mr. Meyer laced his fingers together. "I've met a lot of people in my life, Theo. People who truly examine things — examine themselves, even. And people who don't. I see it in school all the time — the kids who just memorize for the test and the kids who really want to understand.

"You're someone who wants to understand. The road you're choosing is the harder one. But your life will be richer because of it. I guarantee you." He shrugged. "If that makes you feel any better."

Theo looked around the room, his eyes finally landing on the bulletin board of questions. "How come you never put up the answers?"

Mr. Meyer laughed. "There are lots of answers, Theo.

You need to find the ones that make sense to you." He smiled. "But I have a feeling you already know that."

Theo picked up his books. "Thanks, Mr. Meyer. For everything."

"Any time, Theo. I mean that."

Theo headed to the library to look for Dad. In the *Life* magazines, he found pictures of soldiers holding rifles, pushing Vietnamese into a helicopter. The Vietnamese they were fighting looked just like the Vietnamese they were helping. Theo didn't understand how you could tell them apart.

He saw a picture of a tank shooting out a line of flames, setting the jungle on fire, and another of a soldier driving a bulldozer into a jungle house. The house was made of sticks, the roof of grass. The bulldozer crumpled it completely. And then there was a picture of the women and children who had to leave because their whole village was smashed.

What if he turned the page and saw Dad destroying a whole village of little houses? Did the photos Theo was getting developed at the drugstore have pictures like these? He remembered what JeeBee had said: "War is a

terrible thing, Theo. It makes good men do bad things."
And he remembered Dad's words: "I'm starting to think
this whole war was a bad idea." Theo didn't know if he
could bear to see Dad doing anything bad. But he still
couldn't stop looking at the magazines.

On another page, a wounded soldier lay in the mud
with his uniform all bloody; another soldier's head was
bandaged and blood ran down his face. Theo felt sick
to his stomach. What if one of the wounded guys was
Dad? Would that be any easier to look at than a picture
of Dad destroying a village?

Theo pushed the magazines aside. He'd seen enough
guns and blood for one day. He longed to spend time
with the dad who made pancakes and raced little cars.
Maybe if he kept reading, he'd find that dad in the letters. He hurried home to his room, locked his door, and
pulled them out.

Rosemary,
    I wish we didn't have to drop off the same
    kids, day after day. It would be easier if I didn't
    know them.
    We lost this guy named Tony just a couple

days ago. This sweet kid — from Boston, only he called it Baw-ston. You know those funny accents they have up there? He was always talking about the Baw-ston Red Sox.

He'd been injured, and we flew out to pick him up. We'd just landed and our guys were carrying him to the chopper when Charlie chucked one right at us. They blew Tony up and killed one of the guys holding him, too.

If he'd just made it to the chopper, I know I could have saved him.

I don't even want to know their names anymore.

Vince

Hey Kids,

I sure wish I could be with you right now. It gets a little lonely here sometimes.

I'm so glad you're taking ballet lessons, Janet. I can't wait to see you dance! Theo, I can't believe you ate two whole hot dogs. You must be getting big!

It won't be much longer now till I'm home.

Send me two more hugs in your next letter, okay? I really need them!

Dad


Rosemary,

This must have been a beautiful country. Sometimes we'll fly over a rice paddy — the sunlight is sparkling on the water and the rice is so green. There will be an old man walking with his water buffalo and maybe some kids walking with him. So peaceful.

Then we'll fly over a spot our side has bombed — these huge, dead craters, everything blasted away. Or we'll pass over a field our side has sprayed with poison to kill the trees, and I'll wonder how it all used to look before the U. S. of A. came in to <u>help</u>.

Our country says, "Just count." Count how many bad guys we kill, and if we kill more of them than they kill us, then that means we're winning. When I count "bad guys," you know what I see? The same kids. Maybe they're bad

*guys, maybe they're the enemy. But they're the
same dead kids I see on our side. Some of them
don't even have shoes.*

*I don't think we're going to win this war.
I'm not even sure anymore why we got into
it in the first place. When I see an old man
walking with his water buffalo, I keep thinking
he probably doesn't even care who wins, North
Vietnam or South. He just wants it to be over.*

*The whole thing has been a waste.*

*Vince*


*Hey listen, one more thing. I've been thinking
about when I get back to the States, maybe I'll
drive home. You know me — I do my best thinking when I'm driving. We'll be landing in San
Francisco or Oakland, I'm not sure which. But
maybe I'll buy a junker and drive instead of fly.
It should only take me a few days. I really need
a few days of complete silence.*


If only he'd made it back to the States, Theo thought,
he would have driven home and just pulled into the

driveway one day like all the other dads coming home from work.

Rosemary,

I'm not sleeping so good these days. I fall asleep fast. I sleep hard. But then about 2 or 3 in the morning, I have a nightmare that wakes me up.

You know those dreams people have where they're being chased and they're trying to run, but their legs are so heavy they can barely move? My dreams are kind of like that, only in mine the helicopter can't take off. We're at a hot landing zone picking up wounded, and I can hear firing all around us. We have to do it fast, touch down for a few seconds, and then get the hell out of there.

Only in my dream we load up the wounded, but then the chopper shudders and sways, a few feet off the ground, but it won't fly up. And then it shudders again and sinks back down, back into all that firing, with me and the crew and all those wounded just sitting there like dead ducks.

And then I'm awake, sitting bolt upright in my bed, sweating, my heart pounding.

And the thing that keeps me up for the rest of the night is the fact that it would be all my fault. _I'm_ the one who's supposed to fix this bird, keep her running smoothly. If I screw up and she doesn't fly, then it's not just me that eats it — it's everyone else who's riding her, too. . . .

## NEIL AND BUZZ SPENT TWO HOURS

walking around on the moon. But the thing that gets me is that it was at the same time we were fighting the war in Vietnam. The exact same time.

The same second that Neil Armstrong was stepping down onto the surface of the moon, some guy in Vietnam was probably stepping onto a mine and losing his leg, maybe even dying.

The whole two hours that Neil and Buzz were taking those big, bounding steps, there were little houses getting crushed and people getting shot.

It doesn't seem like it should have been happening at the same time.

When Neil and Buzz took off from the moon, they left a plaque behind, signed by them and Mike Collins, and even the president. It said:

HERE MEN FROM THE PLANET EARTH
FIRST SET FOOT UPON THE MOON
JULY 1969, A.D.
WE CAME IN PEACE FOR ALL MANKIND

163

## THEO SLID THE LETTERS BACK

in their hiding place. Maybe Mom hadn't told him and Janet about the letters because they were so horrible — full of people dying and Dad in pain. The more Theo read, the worse he felt. Maybe Mom was just trying to protect him and Janet. Maybe it *was* better to follow her rules, not talk about Dad, act like everything was fine.

He unlocked his door and went downstairs. What would he do if everything were fine? He'd set the table without being asked. He'd even pick some flowers from the garden and put them in a cup. Maybe if he just tried hard enough, everything would *feel* fine.

"My goodness!" Mom said when she got home. "What a beautiful table. There's even flowers!" When she put Theo to work chopping celery, he pretended nothing was wrong.

"Isn't this nice!" Mom said as they sat down to eat.

Theo forced himself to smile.

"Janet, look what a nice job Theo did, setting the table. There's even flowers!"

"Yes, a lovely job," Janet agreed. "That Theodore is a lovely boy."

When Mom dished up the casserole, when Theo buttered his roll, when he drank his milk and shook salt on his peas, he pretended everything was fine. Janet griped about her teachers; Theo pretended to listen. Mom talked about work; Theo pretended to be interested. It made everything so easy! All he had to do was nod.

"You're not eating, Theo," Mom said. "Are you feeling alright?" She put her hand on his forehead. "You're so quiet tonight."

"Probably puberty." Janet shoveled peas into her mouth. "Check his chest for hairs."

Theo tried to force down the food. He ate just enough that he could spread the rest out on his plate and make it look like he'd eaten more. He didn't even have dessert. Mom gave him a worried look as he left the table.

Theo went up to his room and sat down at his desk. He'd studied the launchpad diagram earlier, carefully laying out dozens of model pieces, but now that it was time to actually fit everything together, Theo felt overwhelmed. The instructions were confusing, poorly written with multiple steps.

Janet stuck her head in the doorway. "Don't you dare get sick on me, Theo," she whispered. "I need you to come downtown with me on Saturday."

He heard her door shut, her stereo click on.

He'd just have to work blindly, he decided, try to figure out the first step, and when that was done, the second. Theo opened the tube of glue, the sharp, chemical scent hitting his face and filling the room. As he began to fit the launchpad together, his eyes watered and his stomach felt sour. But he kept working, reminding himself that nothing was confusing and everything was absolutely fine.

"Okay," Mr. Meyer said to the class on Thursday. "You have six more days to finish your projects. How many of you are already done?"

A sea of hands shot up. Theo's stomach clenched.

"Great," Mr. Meyer said. "I've been thinking about what Cynthia said, whether to let you bring your projects in early. And I've decided that we should do that. I think it will help those of you who are stuck get some ideas. So if you're done, bring your project in tomorrow and I'll put them up."

Theo slid down in his seat. What if everyone brought in something tomorrow except him?

Kenny raised his hand. "Hey, Mr. Meyer. I was thinking about something. What if the aliens don't have eyeballs?"

Theo shook his head. It was just like Kenny to ask a question like that. Kenny never took anything seriously.

"Yeah," Rhonda added. "Or ears. I was thinking about that, too. How will they understand the golden record?"

"I've been waiting for someone to ask that," Mr. Meyer said. "What do the rest of you think?"

"Of course they'll have eyeballs," Cynthia scoffed. "How else could they see?"

Kenny shrugged. "But not everything can see. Aren't there fish that live in black caves their whole lives? They can't see."

"But they still have eyeballs," Cynthia persisted. "They just don't work."

"What good are eyeballs that don't work?" Kenny asked. He shot Theo a goofy grin, but Theo ignored it.

Instead, he raised his hand. "The aliens are probably smart — smarter than humans. Maybe they'd invent a machine to see and hear for them."

Mr. Meyer nodded. "Perhaps. The truth is we'll probably never know if one of the golden records ever reaches *anyone*, much less someone or something who'll be able to understand it." He walked over to his desk.

"But maybe the most important thing isn't that someone will understand the golden record. Maybe it's that we made it in the first place." He smiled at the class, then held up a piece of paper. "Last one."

He carried it over to the bulletin board. Such good questions, Theo thought. Only he didn't know how to answer any of them. He still had no idea what to pick for his project.

Mr. Meyer slapped up the last piece of paper: WHAT HAVE WE ACCOMPLISHED?

When the bell rang, Kenny passed by Theo's desk. "Hey, Theo," he said.

When Theo looked up, he noticed Joey and William, standing by the door. They were holding their Boy Scout manuals, waiting for Kenny so they could all go off to Room Five and eat snacks and plan their campout. The one they'd go on with their dads. "Better hurry," Theo said. "Don't want to be late for your meeting."

This time he met Kenny's eyes straight on and saw the confusion and hurt turn to anger. "You're right," Kenny said. "I shouldn't waste my time." He knocked the back of Theo's chair with his leg as he stormed away.

As Theo hurried out of class and to the drugstore, his

stomach grew queasy. He'd never been mean to Kenny before. Theo felt like he was squirming inside, trying to get away from himself. But then his anger welled up. Kenny had it easy.

Theo picked up the envelope of photographs and stuffed them down his shirt, where they stayed, the stiff paper poking his stomach the whole way to the library. Now that he had the photos, he was scared to look. But he forced himself to pull them out.

The photos were black and white: dusty buildings and guys standing in fatigues, a lot with their shirts off.

Then he flipped to another photo and there was Dad, standing next to a helicopter, his hand resting on the nose of the chopper like it was a prize milking cow. There were photos of the helicopter from different angles — side, front, even one where Dad must have climbed inside and taken one out the chopper's big square door.

In the last picture, Dad was sitting on a cot. Was that where he slept? Was that where he had the nightmares?

Theo held the stack of photographs. They showed so little, really — Dad on the base, not Dad in war. What kinds of things might Dad have done or seen while he was fighting? His letters told Theo part of the story. Maybe the magazine photos would tell Theo the rest.

Theo scanned the library shelves — there were only a few volumes left that he hadn't looked at. He set them on the floor and hunkered down next to them.

He opened a magazine and saw a soldier leading away a Vietnamese prisoner splattered in blood. He found another photo of a sniper aiming, ready to fire. There were wounded soldiers being loaded onto a helicopter. Theo flipped past these pictures until he found better ones. A soldier holding a baby. Another laughing with kids. A soldier teaching an old man how to fish. Maybe Dad had done these things, too.

He turned the pages. Here were more soldiers. They were wearing these big striped pajamas. POWs, the article said. Prisoners of War.

Theo froze. What if Dad wasn't MIA? What if he was a POW?

He pushed the magazines aside. He hurried over to the card catalog and found a call number for a whole book on POWs. It said that the POWs got released in 1973. But some people thought that there were still soldiers hidden away in secret prisons.

Maybe Dad was one of them!

Theo could hardly believe it! Mom would be so happy that he had figured it out.

He skimmed the rest of the book. The POWs were locked in cells all by themselves. They weren't allowed to speak to one another — their captors thought they'd plan an escape. So the POWs figured out a way around this. A code, so simple it was perfect:

|   | 1 | 2 | 3 | 4 | 5 |
|---|---|---|---|---|---|
| 1 | A | B | C | D | E |
| 2 | F | G | H | I | J |
| 3 | L | M | N | O | P |
| 4 | Q | R | S | T | U |
| 5 | V | W | X | Y | Z |

Their fingers tapped the wall to spell out each letter. There was no K — the men used a C, instead. So 'H' was two taps — pause — three taps: two rows down, three letters across. And 'I' was two-four. All that tapping, Theo thought, just to say hello. One of the POWs said that sometimes the prison sounded like it was full of woodpeckers.

Theo scribbled down the code. He figured out how to tap his name: 4-4, 2-3, 1-5, 3-4. He knew he couldn't talk to Dad that way. But he wanted to learn it anyway.

Then he hurried home to tell Mom.

# NO MATTER WHAT THE POWs WERE

*tapping, I think this is what they really wanted*
*to know:*

* _ * * *
* _ *
* * * _ * * *


* * * * * _ * * * *
* * * _ * * * *
* * * * _ * * * * *


* * _ * * *
* _ * * * * *
* _ *
* * * * _ * *


* * * _ * *
* _ * * * * *

## THEO PACED THE WHOLE HOUSE,

waiting for someone, anyone, to get home. When he heard the kitchen door open, he raced downstairs. Janet walked in, holding a brown paper bag of groceries. She grinned at Theo. "I talked Mom into getting two kinds of ice cream: mint chocolate chip —"

"I figured it out!" he cried.

Mom walked in, holding two more bags. "Figured what out, honey?"

"I know where Dad is."

The bags slid from Mom's hands. She managed to hold on to one, but the other dropped to the floor. "I don't *believe* it!"

"I know! Isn't it *great*? *I figured it out!*" Theo rushed on. "He's a POW. Now all we have to do is get him out."

Janet's mouth fell open.

"Oh my God." Mom fumbled her grocery bag over to the kitchen table, her gait uncertain. She sank into her chair.

"Oh, Theo," Janet murmured.

"Don't worry, Mom." Theo scooped up the other

**173**

grocery bag, its side split, and set it on the kitchen counter. "Now that we know where he is, all we have to do is get the government to get him out."

He hurried over to Mom and sat down next to her, but Janet hung back. She slunk over to the kitchen counter and set her bag on it. Then she hugged her arms to her chest.

Mom's hands were pressed against the tabletop. She steadied herself and took a deep breath. "Theo, listen to me. They were all released, years ago." She put an icy hand on his arm. "I'm sorry, honey. But . . . I don't think we're ever going to find out what happened to him. We all need to try and move on."

Theo flushed. "You think he's dead, don't you?"

Janet gasped.

Mom cradled her forehead in her hand. "Oh my God." Suddenly she slapped her hands down on the tabletop and groaned.

"You have to tell him, Mom," Janet said.

Mom froze.

Janet hugged herself a little closer. "Theo, Dad's not a POW." She shook her head. "He's not even MIA."

Mom looked up. "You know?"

"I heard you and JeeBee arguing a few years ago,"

Janet told her. Then she said to Theo, "JeeBee thought we should know, but Mom didn't want to tell us yet."

"Tell us what?" Theo sat up.

Janet sighed. "Dad came back the summer he was supposed to. He landed in California and called here, but we weren't home, so he called JeeBee. He told her he was buying a car and driving home. But then he never showed up."

Theo's head felt foggy. "I don't understand."

Mom's face was wooden, her eyes dead. "I called Highway Patrol for days, to make sure there wasn't an accident. But there wasn't."

"He came back?"

Janet nodded. "He came back to the States. He just didn't come back to us."

"Why didn't you *tell* me?" Theo cried. But as soon as he asked, he knew the answer.

Mom closed her eyes as the tears spilled down her cheeks. Janet looked at the floor.

"I still don't understand. Why didn't he come home?" Theo persisted.

Mom slumped down further in her seat. "He sent me a letter a few days after he got back to the States. He said he needed a little time. He said he couldn't explain it, but he needed to try to understand what he'd been through, and that he'd call soon." She shook her head. "But he never did."

"So he's still trying to figure it out? The war?"

"I don't know what he's thinking," Mom blurted out. "And I don't care!" She paused and took a breath. Then she reached out and put her hand on Theo's arm again. "I'm so sorry. I should have told you a long time ago." She turned to Janet. "Both of you." Then her face grew hard again. "He made his choice. But he's never going to hurt us again."

She rose abruptly. "And we're going to be just fine. Look how strong and beautiful my two children are." Her eyes filled with tears, but she shook them away. She planted a firm kiss on the top of Theo's head, then one on Janet's. "We'll be fine, all by ourselves."

She walked over to the split grocery bag. As she started to unload it, food spilled out onto the countertop. She examined a carton of eggs. "Cracked," she announced. "Well, we'll just have scrambled eggs for dinner. See? We're fine." She turned back to the groceries and began to put them away.

In a daze, Theo walked out of the kitchen and up to his room. He pulled out the letters and looked through the stack. He realized there was only one more letter to read.

Rosemary,

This is a quick note. Sorry I haven't written much lately.

I'm still here. Still in one piece.

I tried to find out what date I'm landing, but I can't get any info. I may just have to call you when I get to San Francisco. I still want to drive home. I need some time to think. Or maybe not do any thinking at all. Don't be mad — I want to see you and the kids. I just need a couple days of nothing but highway.

Well, we're heading out on patrol early in the morning. Guess the army wants to get their money's worth before they ship me home.

Not that any of it's worth a damn. I've been asking myself what the hell we've accomplished over here, but I still don't have an answer. Maybe I'll figure that out while I'm driving home.

I'm going to try and get some sleep. Early day tomorrow.

Vince

Theo tucked the letters back in their spot and lay down on the bed. What questions did Dad ask himself when he started driving home? Was he still searching for the answers?

When Mom called Theo down to dinner later, Janet was already in the living room with her plate. Mom never let them watch TV during dinner, but tonight she didn't say a word. She and Theo dished up their plates and sat down on the couch to watch, too.

After dinner Janet headed straight up to her room, even though it was her night to load the dishwasher. But Mom still didn't say anything. She loaded it herself and then went upstairs.

Theo tried to watch TV, but he couldn't concentrate on even the dumbest shows. A while later, Mom came down to tell him to get ready for bed. Theo noticed some chocolate in the corner of her mouth.

He brushed his teeth, walked back into his room, and shut the door behind him. For the first time ever, he went to bed with his door closed. But he knew no one would notice — Janet's and Mom's doors were closed, too.

# DID YOU KNOW THAT WHEN THE

first astronauts came home from the moon, they were quarantined?

NASA wasn't sure if it was safe for them to be near people. What if they'd caught some weird disease that doctors couldn't cure? What if it was contagious?

So the astronauts stayed in this science lab that was completely sealed off from the rest of the world. They couldn't even visit their families. They could only wave at them through a big glass window.

The only other people sealed up in the lab were doctors and scientists. The scientists took some of the moon dust that the astronauts had brought home and injected it into some mice. Then they watched to see if the mice got sick.

For almost three weeks the astronauts stayed shut up in the lab, looking out the big window and waiting to hear if the mice died. Then the scientists killed the mice and did an autopsy to see if their insides were messed up.

Doesn't seem very fair to the mice.

If the mice had gotten some weird moon disease, I wonder how the astronauts would have felt. Would they have stayed in their rooms, waiting to die, too? Would they have thought the trip was worth it?

**WHEN THEO CAME INTO CLASS**
the next day, Mr. Meyer had cleared all the questions from his big bulletin board. Across the top, he'd written: THIS IS EARTH, and now kids were starting to display their projects.

Ever since Mr. Meyer had first announced the assignment, Theo had been looking forward to seeing what everyone would bring in. But now he felt nothing, like he was walking around on some alien planet where gravity was a little bit heavier and everyone spoke some language he couldn't quite understand.

He scanned the bulletin board. There was a picture of the ocean. Another one of a family sitting around a table loaded with food. A picture of two kids, one black and one white, playing together. A picture of a church. A picture of a forest. One of a piano. Another of a chocolate bar. A baseball game, a bird flying, a dinosaur. Joey had even put up a picture of himself, grinning hugely like *he* was the most important thing about Earth.

Theo still had no idea what he was going to choose.

Near the center was a picture of Buster, sitting on Kenny's dad's underwear, his big square head thrown back in a miserable howl.

Theo looked over at Kenny, joking around with some guys. They were looking at the bulletin board and laughing. After school he watched them walk out together, his heart sinking. Kenny never even looked in Theo's direction.

Theo trudged home and into the house. No one was home. Good. He didn't feel like talking to anyone, anyway. He hauled himself upstairs and dumped his stuff on the bed. He felt like punching something. Breaking something. He stomped downstairs. He wanted to bash the hammer into a million nails.

He yanked open the garage door so hard it crashed into the wall.

Janet shrieked and spun around. She was by the workbench, clutching a little box to her chest. "Theo! You scared me!"

"Janet? What are you doing out here?"

She held out the box of nails. "Didn't you ever notice that you never run out?"

Theo hadn't. "Thanks," he said.

Janet nodded.

As he watched her dump the nails into the nail jar, a cold, sick feeling settled in his stomach. "You were right. If Dad cared about us, he'd be here."

Janet picked up the hammer and carried it over to him. "Here."

Theo actually felt like a space cadet when Janet woke him up the next morning. "Why do *I* have to go?" he groaned.

"I already *told* you." She pulled a shirt from one drawer, socks from another, then grabbed his jeans from the back of his chair. "Mom'd *kill* me if she found out I went downtown by myself." She threw the clothes at Theo.

"Can we at least go to the Air and Space Museum, after?"

"Just get dressed, Theo!"

When he stumbled downstairs, there was already a bowl of cereal on the table. "Eat," Janet said. "We're leaving in ten minutes."

"Where's Mom?"

"Work." The last few weeks of school were especially busy for her, and she sometimes had to go in on Saturdays. Janet scribbled a note and put it on the table.

Mom,

*I'm helping Theo with his science project.*

Love,

Janet

His stomach clenched. The *Voyager* project was due in four days and he still had no idea what to choose. "Look, Janet. I don't think I can go. I have to work on my project."

Janet looked stricken. "Theo, you *promised*!"

He hadn't, not really. But she seemed desperate.

"Please, Theo? I need you!"

Theo sighed. He'd have to do his project tomorrow—he'd spend all day on it till he figured *something* out. "Okay," he finally agreed.

"Thanks!" She grabbed the newspaper and raced upstairs.

Theo had only eaten half his cereal when Janet stormed back in, her big fringed purse slung over her shoulder. She took the bowl from under Theo's spoon.

"I'm still eating!"

"You're full." She dumped the cereal down the sink. "Come on, Theo!"

He'd barely put on his shoes when she dragged

him out the front door, turning right instead of left. "Where are we going?" Theo said. "The bus stop is the other way."

Janet started to run. "We can't use the *same* bus stop as JeeBee. We have to get on *before* her, so she won't see us."

"Won't she see us when she gets on the bus?" Theo struggled to keep up. Janet was fast.

"I have it all figured out. Now hurry!"

They arrived at the bus stop just as the bus was pulling up. Janet practically tugged the shirt off Theo's back as they stumbled up the bus steps. She paid the fare. Theo sat down behind the driver.

"Not *here*." She yanked him down the aisle, lurching as the bus pulled back into traffic. "There." She pointed to the back of the bus.

"Okay, but quit yelling at me."

"Sorry." Janet pushed him onto a seat in the back and sat down next to him. She pulled a newspaper from her purse and opened it up in front of their faces. "Hold the other side. I made a little hole so I can see JeeBee." When the bus pulled in to the next stop, Janet stuck her face up to the newspaper and peered through the opening. "There she is!"

"Why didn't you make *me* a hole, too?"

Janet turned to him. She had newsprint smudged on her nose. "I didn't want to be *conspicuous*." She turned back to the peephole again.

"What's she doing? Let me see!"

Janet sighed heavily, but slid the paper over his way. Theo peeked through. There was JeeBee, on the bench behind the driver. She looked tiny.

The bus droned on, finally pulling up at the transfer stop. It always waited here for a few minutes while people from other buses got on. Theo peeked out at JeeBee from behind the paper, and suddenly he felt a flash of anger toward her. All this time she'd known that Dad chose not to come home. Why would she want Theo to learn about Dad now, after what he'd done?

Theo watched as a young mom holding a baby in one arm and a stroller in the other struggled up the steps and sat down next to JeeBee.

Why had JeeBee wanted to talk about Dad? Maybe, Theo realized as he watched JeeBee play with the baby, because she knew that one day Theo would find out. Maybe she thought that the better Theo understood his dad and what the war had done to him, the better he might be able to understand why his dad didn't come home. "He came back to the States. He just didn't come back to us," Janet had said. Now, watching the baby smile and reach his pudgy hand toward JeeBee, Theo realized that Dad hadn't come back to her, either.

When the bus merged into traffic again, Janet reached into her purse and pulled out a pack of Juicy Fruit. "Sorry you didn't get to finish breakfast." Awkwardly, she unwrapped a piece with her free hand. "Here. Thanks for coming."

Theo didn't really like Juicy Fruit, but Janet almost never gave him anything. He popped it in his mouth.

Soon the bus made its first stops on the National Mall, the long grassy park capped by the Lincoln Memorial and the Capitol. Janet plastered her face to the hole in the paper. "When JeeBee gets off, we need to see which way she walks."

Theo peeked around the side of the paper. Near the Capitol, JeeBee reached up and pulled the cord. The bell chimed *ding*!

"Theo, get back behind here!" Janet whispered.

Out the window Theo saw JeeBee step down off the bus. In the swirl of passengers and tourists, she looked even tinier. Without a glance back at the bus, she took off.

"She's going down Constitution Avenue."

"Yeah, I saw." Janet snatched the paper away. The bus lurched forward, turning north, and Janet's hand shot up to pull the cord. They got off at the next stop. Janet reached in her purse and pulled out a green baseball cap and sunglasses. "Put these on."

Theo studied the cap. "Where'd you get this?"

"A kid at school." She put on a hat, too, a blue one that Theo didn't recognize.

"Which kid?"

"It doesn't matter, Theodore! Just wear it." Then she handed him a map. "Hold this up in front of your face."

Theo unfolded it. "It's for Baltimore."

"Yeah, I know. I couldn't find the D.C. one." She pulled a big red bandanna out of her purse and stuck it in front of her face, like she was blowing her nose. "C'mon!"

Theo hurried after her, the map covering his mouth and nose. "Janet, we look stupid!" he complained, but she just kept walking.

Lots of people passed by: A woman wearing a big sunhat, pushing a stroller. A family with three little kids, all wearing matching shirts. Two blocks later they caught sight of JeeBee. "I don't see a beauty parlor anywhere," Janet noted. They followed JeeBee as she turned a corner, leaving the Capitol behind them. The tourists began to thin out. Theo and Janet hugged the walls of the buildings.

"Where's she going?" Theo asked.

"I don't know."

There weren't many people on the streets now. The buildings seemed more run-down. "I don't think Mom would like us being here," Theo said.

"I know." Janet hooked her hand around Theo's arm.

Every once in a while, JeeBee said hello to someone she saw on the street. "How does she know all these people?" Janet murmured.

"She must come here every week," Theo answered. Just then, JeeBee walked up the steps of a tan, two-story building.

Janet ducked into an alley between two apartment complexes, pulling Theo in behind her. Then she peeked around the corner at the tan building.

"What's in there?" Theo asked.

Janet shook her head. "I can't tell from here."

A man passed by, giving them a strange look. "Are you lost?"

"No, sir. We're waiting for our grandma." Janet smiled politely. Theo marveled at how she always managed to tell the truth, even when she was lying.

She kept watch, but Theo sat on the ground, leaning against the brick wall, trying to get comfortable. He drew designs with his finger into the sandy grit on the ground — big Xs that he realized reminded him of helicopter blades. He looked up at Janet, her face frozen in concentration as she watched the building. "I don't remember Dad," he heard himself say. "Barely at all."

She whipped her head around. "Why does it matter? He's forgotten about us. Just forget about him." She turned back to the building.

"I can't," Theo said. "I can't stop thinking about him." He took a deep breath. "Sometimes JeeBee tells me stories about him."

Janet scowled. She glared at the building, chewing on her thumbnail. But then after a moment, she asked, "What does she say?"

Theo told Janet all JeeBee had said, about Dad fixing cars, making cookies, eating clay. About how he liked to putter in the garage . . .

"I remember him doing that," Janet mumbled.

He told her how Dad was curious and liked to figure

things out. "JeeBee said I'm a lot like him. Quiet, like him, and good with my hands. I bet if you asked her she could tell you how *you're* like —"

Janet silenced him with her stare. "I'm not like him at all."

She turned back to the building. Suddenly she grabbed Theo's arm, yanked him to his feet, and pulled him down the alleyway. "JeeBee just came out the door!" They ducked behind a rusty Dumpster that smelled of garbage and old beer, and watched her pass by.

"Should we follow her?" Theo whispered.

"In a sec." Janet stuffed her bandanna back in her purse. "C'mon. I want to check that place out first."

The building was in better shape than the other buildings on the block. Theo read the sign by the door. "It's a youth center." He could hear the sound of kids playing in back.

Janet stood for a moment, reading the sign. Then she shrugged. "We're youth." She walked up the steps.

"Janet! Wait!" But when she didn't, he scrambled to catch up.

They pushed open the door, walking past the bulletin boards that flanked each side of the hallway, toward the sound of typing. They followed it to a small office. Inside a large woman typed at a desk. She seemed surprised to see them, but she smiled. "Can I help you?"

Janet walked right up to her. "Yes, ma'am. We're youth. We wondered what this place was."

The woman frowned, slightly. "Do you live in this neighborhood?" Through the office window, Theo watched a little girl run by, holding a ball.

"Yes, ma'am. We live nearby."

Theo looked over at Janet. Nearby? Only if you sat on a bus for an hour.

But Janet was flashing her most encouraging smile.

"I see." The woman reached over and picked up a pamphlet. "Well, we're a youth center for the kids who live in the Capitol Hill area. We have various programs — - recreational, educational. You can read about them in this pamphlet."

Janet took it. "You have teachers here?"

"Well, yes. We call them 'mentors' but they do some teaching, too."

Janet nodded, but the woman was frowning again. "You said you're from around here? Exactly which street do you live on?"

"Just over there." Janet took Theo's arm. "Well, we

better go. We have lots of youth-type stuff to do." And she pulled Theo out of the room.

"Let's see if we can catch up with JeeBee." Janet rushed toward the front door, but Theo was distracted by the bulletin boards on each side of the hallway. He stopped to look at the newspaper clippings and photographs: Kids and a couple of skinny teenagers, playing basketball. A group of boys and a hippie with a bushy brown beard, standing by a truck with its hood open. A little girl painting a picture with a big fat paintbrush. More kids —

"It's JeeBee!" Theo said. There she was, smiling with a bunch of kids who were all blowing big pink bubbles. OUR NEWEST VOLUNTEER, someone had written on a little sign.

Janet hurried back to look at the picture. "That explains the gumballs. . . ." She turned to Theo and nodded. "Self-fulfillment. I told you JeeBee wanted to reach her full potential."

They found JeeBee in another photo, sitting on an old red couch, reading a book to a group of kids gathered around her. "But why would she keep it a secret?" Theo asked.

Janet shrugged. "It's kind of a bad neighborhood. . . .

Maybe she's afraid we'd think she's too old — she is sixty, after all."

Theo heard the noise of a chair squeaking, then heavy footsteps. The woman was coming out of her office. He grabbed Janet's arm and they hurried out the door.

They began to jog, scanning each side street they passed. "Do you see her anywhere?" Janet asked.

"No."

They didn't slow down until they reached the Capitol. Tourists were milling, but there was no sign of JeeBee.

"Rats," Janet said.

"Well, at least you know where she goes every Saturday. Let's go to the Air and Space Museum."

Janet grabbed his arm. "Hang on. There's somewhere we need to go first. It'll just take a second."

She led him down First Street, hurrying by the Capitol without even looking, but Theo slowed to check things out. He watched a woman holding a microphone, talking to three guys in fancy suits while a television camera recorded the interviews.

"C'mon, Theo." Janet pulled him away. Soon, they were at the steps of a huge building, with arches and pillars and a row of stone faces looking down at them.

"What's this?" Theo asked.

"The Library of Congress. I looked up the address this morning."

They walked into the building. "Why are we here?"

"So later, if Mom asks where we were, I can tell her we went to the library." She turned around to leave. "Okay, let's go."

But Theo saw a sign, listing the displays. "Wait, I want to see something."

"*The-o*, this is a *library*. It's boring in here."

"Hang on." He walked up the steps into the most beautiful room he'd ever seen, from the marble floor beneath him to the top of the gold-domed ceiling.

Even Janet was impressed. "Wow."

Theo hurried toward the display area. There was an exhibit on George Washington and another on sharks. But the one he really wanted to see was called "Mars: Reality and Fantasy."

The "reality" part was photographs of ruddy boulders and dusty plateaus. But the "fantasy" part was new to Theo: H. G. Wells's *The War of the Worlds*, about Martians invading Earth. Theo looked at the illustration of a Martian emerging from its spaceship — oily black tentacles rising out of the charred pit.

"Oh, nice picture of you," Janet said, peering over his shoulder.

Why did people always assume that creatures from outer space would try to hurt us? Theo wondered. If he heard that Martians had landed, he'd try to be like the guy on the *Pioneer* plaque: standing quietly, waving hello. Only Theo was quite sure he'd be wearing clothes.

Janet sighed heavily. "Come on, let's go look at your stupid rockets, you airhead."

They walked to the grassy Mall, where all the museums were. The Air and Space Museum was the long, marble building that looked like a row of cereal boxes.

Inside the light, airy entrance were planes, hanging from the ceiling just like in Theo's room. But these weren't models; they were actual aircraft: The Wright Brothers' *Flyer*, which Orville flew for twelve whole seconds at Kitty Hawk. The *Spirit of St. Louis*, which Charles Lindbergh flew solo across the Atlantic. When Theo looked up at them, he could see blue sky through the glass ceiling.

But that was just the start. On the floor stood the *Gemini 4* spacecraft Edward White had emerged from to be the first American to walk in space. And there, resting peacefully nearby, was the *Apollo 11* command module — the "mother ship" that had carried the first astronauts safely home from the moon.

Theo had seen it twice before, but he still couldn't believe how tiny it was. You'd hardly be able to move in there, Theo thought. He examined the honeycombed heat shield — ashy gray, blackened in spots from the intense heat of reentry.

His favorite display was the sliver of moon rock you could touch. Theo rubbed it until it grew warm beneath his finger. *He was touching the moon! The actual . . .*

"Theodore . . . it's boring in here! Let's go!"

"Wait!" He couldn't leave without seeing the *Apollo* stuff.

"*The-o!*"

He hurried off, not turning around to see if Janet was following. She wouldn't leave without him, or at least, he didn't *think* she would.

Incredible. A lunar landing module, just like the kind Neil and Buzz took down to the surface. Space suits covered with moon dust. Freeze-dried meals like they'd eaten during flight. Even Mike Collins's toothbrush he'd taken with him on —

"*The-o!* I'm *starving!*"

Theo realized that he was, too. He'd only had that

half-bowl of cereal, hours ago. Still, it killed him to leave — he knew he'd never talk Janet into coming back. He took one last look and sighed. "Okay."

Outside the sun was bright. Janet pulled Theo across the grassy Mall. "Let's find some hot dogs or something."

There were little stands selling T-shirts, American flags, bags of popcorn. Theo saw lots of families, moms handing out snacks and dads with cameras around their necks, carrying tired little kids. "Did we ever come downtown with Mom and Dad?"

"Once, that I remember." Janet walked slower. "To see the big elephant."

Theo knew what she meant. Inside the Museum of Natural History was this huge elephant they'd stuffed so it looked like it was walking across a sandy bank in Africa.

Janet's pace slowed until she was barely moving. "Mom wanted to go upstairs to see the gems and minerals, but Dad stayed downstairs with us. He kept telling Mom, 'You can go look at some dumb old jewels if you want. We're staying *right here* — with the *elephant*. And the *dinosaurs*.' We kept taking turns on Dad's shoulders so we could be almost as tall as the *elephant*. And the *dinosaurs*."

Theo tried to remember, but he couldn't. "I want to go there after lunch."

Janet nodded.

Up ahead was another stand. Theo could smell the spicy, juicy scent of fat hot dogs cooking. His stomach growled loudly.

"Hang on." Janet reached in her pocket and pulled out a handful of money. She set aside enough for the bus ride home. That left — Theo counted it quickly — $2.88.

"Two dollars and eighty-eight cents? That's all we have for lunch?"

Janet shrugged. "That's all that was in your money can."

"Janet!"

"What? You didn't want to *starve*, did you?" She walked over to the man. A hot dog, soda, and chips was $1.50, so for two lunches they were twelve cents short, but Janet harangued him until he gave in — probably just to shut her up, Theo thought as he squirted on mustard. Sometimes having Janet around had its benefits.

They sat in the shade of a big tree and ate, watching the tourists. A group of teenagers passed by, laughing and horsing around. Theo swallowed hard. He and Kenny used to horse around like that.

"So what *are* you going to do for your *Voyager* thing?" Janet asked.

Theo was surprised she asked. He hadn't thought she cared. "I haven't figured it out yet." He watched more tourists wander down the sidewalk. "What do *you* think is the most important thing on Earth?"

Janet wiped some mustard from the corner of her mouth. "That's easy: family. You and Mom and JeeBee." Then she blushed and said, "What?!" and Theo realized he was sitting there with his mouth hanging open.

Janet stood and brushed off the seat of her pants. "Oh, don't let it go to your head, Theodore. C'mon."

They walked to the "elephant museum," as Theo heard a little kid call it, draining their sodas at the door. It was cool and dim inside, voices echoing off the marbled pillars all the way up to the domed ceiling.

Theo walked up to the elephant. He'd loved it since he was little — its wrinkled trunk and flappy ears, its stained tusks and dusty feet. It seemed incredibly wise.

Near Theo stood a little boy staring straight up at the elephant, towering overhead. "Pretty big, huh?" the boy's dad said. The boy tilted his head back so far that his baseball cap slipped off, but he didn't even notice. The dad picked it up, then stood quietly, waiting until his son was through looking.

Theo blinked, feeling the burn of new tears. He turned and saw Janet standing beside him. He looked back at the father and son. "It's not fair."

"No." Janet put her hand on Theo's shoulder. "It's not."


On the bus ride home later, Theo found himself getting so sleepy that his head bobbed against Janet's shoulder.

She was murmuring phrases from the youth center pamphlet. Theo listened while he fell in and out of sleep. "'Helping the youth in our nation's capital,'" Janet read. "'Helping build the future of the nation — today.'"

Later that night, Theo sat in bed, looking out the window. The moon was full and bright, making shadows on the lawn. Maybe that really was the best thing to choose for his *Voyager* project, Theo decided: Man on the Moon.

Theo pictured the space suits and moon rovers he'd seen only a few hours ago. Was it really possible that one day he'd go there himself?

He thought back to what JeeBee had said when she'd

given him the atlas — that it was just the map, that he'd have to chart his own course when he got there.

Theo got up, grabbed his flashlight, binoculars, and moon atlas, and climbed back into bed. He opened the atlas, aimed the flashlight on it, and studied the drawing.

He'd land in the Sea of Tranquility and add his footprints to the ones that were already there. He'd climb into his lunar rover and cross the face of the moon. He'd circle around Copernicus, then head into the Ocean of Storms. He'd cruise down the moon's western edge, stopping whenever he felt like it. He'd take his time. Then he'd travel on to explore the far side. But before he did, there was one more stop he'd make on the way.

Theo turned off the flashlight and lay down. He put his hands behind his head and thought back over the day: the long bus ride, following JeeBee and learning her secret, the pictures of her on the youth center walls. And then the visit to the museum where he'd touched the moon.

But something was bugging him — a feeling that he wasn't seeing something important. What was he missing?

And then Theo knew. He felt it hard, like a blow to the chest: the pictures on the youth center walls.

The group of boys gathered around the truck with its hood open. . . .

And the hippie.

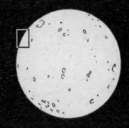

EINSTEIN

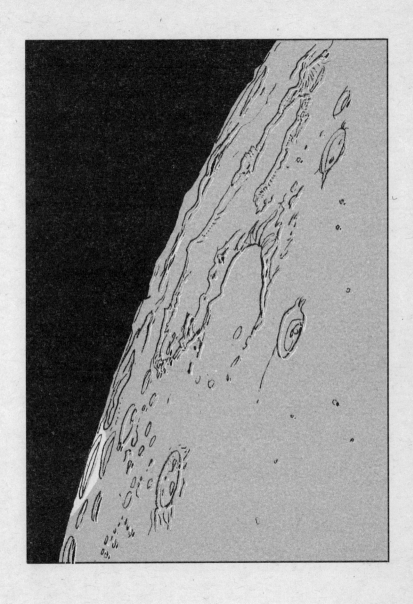

## FOR A MOMENT THEO HAD PAN-

icked. He'd stood in his room Sunday morning, holding his empty money can, wondering how he could buy a bus ticket when Janet had cleaned him out the day before. But then he'd remembered the birthday cards on his desk. He'd never taken out the twelve dollar bills from his mom. He shoved the money in his jacket pocket along with a photo of Dad, standing by the helicopter in Vietnam.

Now he was on the bus, feeling it lurch as it pulled away from the transfer stop and drove the final stretch into D.C.

Theo sank down deeper in his seat. Mom would be furious if she found out he was going downtown by himself. He'd told her he was going to Kenny's. He just hoped she wouldn't call there. He wasn't sure Kenny would cover for him if she did.

Theo squirmed, feeling all hot — his mom would be so mad if she found out he lied. Then he felt his anger rise. *She'd* been lying to *him* for five years, hadn't she? What right would *she* have to get mad?

When the bus got downtown, he headed toward

the Capitol dome. The sidewalks weren't crowded on a Sunday morning. The streets felt pretty empty when he neared the youth center.

He didn't know what he was going to do when he got there. Everything felt too big to figure out. He saw the tan building up ahead, and his stomach twisted. His hands started to sweat. He pushed himself forward, up the steps to the front door. It was locked. Theo peered through the glass to the dark hallway inside.

Now what was he supposed to do? He should have looked at the pamphlet before he left home. He should have guessed the youth center might be closed on Sundays.

Theo felt himself beginning to cry. Stupid. Stupid. He wanted to kick in the door. He sat down on the steps, the image of the hippie filling his mind: standing with his tools, surrounded by kids, teaching them how to fix the truck in front of the garage.

The truck in front of the garage!

Theo stood, looking up and down the block. He didn't see any garage. Maybe the garage was in back?

He hurried around the corner. Halfway down the street was a beat-up alleyway filled with scraggly weeds and the remnants of hopscotch and foursquare drawn with chalk. On the back wall of the youth center, someone had painted a mural of a big rainbow.

Theo heard voices. He slunk up against the wall and crept toward them.

And there it was, just like in the picture: the truck with its hood open. Six boys, some Theo's age, gathered around the hippie with his long brown hair and bushy beard. He held a socket wrench and pointed at the engine. "When we finish, it'll run a lot better," Theo heard him say.

Theo watched the boys crowd around the engine. He could feel them wanting to hold the wrench, get their fingers greasy black, take something broken and make it work.

A boy said something Theo couldn't hear. Theo watched the hippie smile, heard the hippie laugh. Hadn't Theo heard that laugh before?

"Hey!" Theo shouted without even realizing it. The blood rushed to his face as they all turned to stare. But as soon as he looked in the hippie's eyes, Theo knew for sure. It was Dad. He'd never been more sure of anything in his life.

Dad's eyes grew wide. His jaw dropped. "Theo?"

"You've been here the *whole time*, only an hour away?" Theo seethed. "How come you help all these *other* kids?"

"Theo, I can explain. . . ."

"What about *us*? WHAT ABOUT *ME*?" Theo screamed.

Then he ran.

Theo's side was cramping and his breath was ragged by the time he stopped. He was almost to the bus stop. He saw one pull up and he dashed across the street to it, hearing brakes squeal.

He lurched up the steps and threw himself down on a seat, smearing his shirt across his face to dry his tears. He glared out the window — just in time to see Dad racing toward the corner, shouting and flagging the bus driver, and then his hands falling to his sides as the bus pulled away.

It took Theo almost four hours to get home. He'd jumped on the wrong bus, and by the time he'd figured that out, he was well into Maryland. He'd had to wait for another bus and transfer twice, and walk almost a mile in between.

When he finally shot off the last bus, he stormed toward home. As he turned the corner to his street, he saw Janet sitting on the porch steps, her cheek resting on her knees. She leaped up and ran to meet him. "Are you okay?" Her eyes were red.

"I found Dad."

"I know. He called JeeBee after you ran off, and she came right over. Mom and JeeBee drove around for hours, looking for you. They just got back."

"Where are they?"

"Waiting by the phone in case you call."

Theo hurried forward, but Janet put her hand on his arm and slowed him down. "Mom's pretty mad."

Theo marched up the steps and into the house. "So am I."

He yanked open the door, Janet following behind. Mom and JeeBee jerked up out of their chairs. "Theo, thank God you're alright!" Mom cried. "We were so worried!" She rushed over and hugged him. "I can't believe you did that, Theo! You could have been killed!"

Theo pushed her away. "You lied to us. You've been

lying for *years*! Why would you let us think he was MIA when he's been living in D.C.? Why would you do that?"

"I swear I just found out where he was. JeeBee just told me!"

"A week ago," JeeBee protested. "When Vince asked to see you kids and your mother said no —"

Theo was thunderstruck. He reeled on Mom, feeling rage fill his body as he realized what she'd done. "You didn't even *ask* us? You didn't even *care* what we'd want? Why do *you* get to choose? He's our dad."

He turned to Janet, pulled the photo out of his pocket, and thrust it at her. "Dad wrote us letters, too. He wrote them to *us*. Mom's been hiding them all this time."

"You searched in my room?" Mom said.

"I know everything! About the letters and his sketchbook and your stupid candy bars! You just keep lying to us!"

Mom began to cry, but Theo didn't care.

He wheeled around and strode toward the stairs, passing The Ladies perched on their shelf. Before he realized what he was doing, his arm swept several to the ground. Theo heard a splintering sound as he rushed on.

He ran up the stairs, Janet on his heels, and burst into his room with his messy desk and his unmade bed and clothes on the floor and the seven model aircraft, hovering over all. He knew if he didn't keep moving, he'd explode.

"Theo . . ." Janet said.

He reached up and grabbed Navy Helicopter 66, the one that had recovered the *Apollo* astronauts after splashdown. The string from the ceiling stretched and then broke. Theo dropped the helicopter and stomped on it, hearing plastic crack. It took a few tries to bash through the cockpit. But the Wright Brothers' *Flyer* crumpled as soon as he placed his foot on the paper-thin struts. The B-52 bomber's silver wings snapped off neatly. The Vostok rocket split right up the middle. He crushed the *Mercury-Atlas*. The *Bleriot XI* shattered completely.

He pulled down the last plane, an F-86 Sabre jet — the first plane he'd ever made, the one he'd made with Dad when he was only five.

Theo held it in his hands for a moment, looking at the bright yellow racing stripes painted on its wings and fuselage. Up close, he could see how sloppy the stripes were, like they were painted by a little kid. And now he remembered — *really* remembered: Dad held the plane while Theo painted.

"Theo. No." His mom stood in the doorway, weeping. "Please."

Janet took the plane from his hands, led him to the bed, and sat down next to him.

Mom hugged herself in the doorway. JeeBee stood behind her, her hand covering her mouth.

"I should have told you last week," Mom said. "I should have asked you if you wanted to see him. I was just scared . . . it would hurt you too much." She came and knelt beside them. "I didn't mean to lie to you for so long. It just seemed easier, after a while, to pretend he'd never existed."

Theo turned to JeeBee. "How long have you known where he was?"

"Just a few weeks," she said. "Truly."

"Did he say why?" Theo asked. "Did he say why he didn't come home?"

JeeBee stood in the doorway like she wasn't sure she should come into the room. "He's tried to explain it to me, Theo. He did it for you."

Mom snorted. "Right."

"He said when he got back from the war, he was wound up so tight, the smallest thing set him off," JeeBee said. "He said it was like there was this . . . this huge *roar* inside him, and every time he opened his mouth, it tried to come out." She looked down and said quietly, "He was afraid . . . you'd be scared of him."

Theo tried to imagine what it would have been like, living with a dad like that. Would he have been scared of his own dad? Would it still have been better than having him gone?

"He's been trying all this time to come home," JeeBee said.

"Not hard enough," Mom muttered.

"But he *did* try," Theo said. "Last week. And you said *no*. What if he disappears again? What if that was our only chance?"

Mom started crying again. "I didn't know if you were ready. I was trying to protect you."

Janet nodded slowly. "And yourself. You were trying to protect yourself."

Mom bowed her head. "I was so hurt when he didn't come home. And so angry."

JeeBee stepped forward and knelt down on the floor by the shattered models. "Vince feels terrible about what he did." She shook her head. "He moved to D.C. a few weeks ago because he wants to try and make it up to you all. If you'll give him a chance." She took a deep breath and let it out slowly. "What do you think? Do you want to see your dad again?"

Theo looked at the models, broken on the floor. The F-86 Sabre jet still lay on Janet's lap. He held out his hand, and she placed it on his palm.

Theo squeezed, feeling the rigid plastic give under his pressure until a crack appeared down each side. The plane was just a little, hollow shell. He could crush it in an instant and toss it in the garbage like a piece of trash.

Or, he thought, turning the plane over and over in his hands, he could try to fix it.

**THERE ARE RULES IN SCIENCE AND**
reasons for everything, even the things that don't
seem to make sense. Space seems so big you'd think
you could never understand it. But you can. All the
rules work, even the ones that seem like they
shouldn't.

Take Einstein. He spent his life thinking about
time and speed and space. What he figured out
doesn't make sense: The faster you go, the slower
time goes.

We can never travel at the speed of light, but it's
not because we can't design a powerful enough rocket.
At the speed of light, time stops. You're on a rocket
going faster and faster, but time is moving slower
and slower, until you're moving so fast that you're not
moving at all.

It doesn't make sense, but it's true anyway.

Einstein's crater is on the very outer edge of
the moon, but the moon wobbles a little bit each
month. Sometimes you can see Einstein, but

sometimes it's slipped over to the far side of the moon.

The far side never faces Earth. No matter how good a telescope you have, you can never see it. The only way to understand it is to go there.

## THEO SAT ON HIS BED, HOLDING

the letter that was waiting for him when he came home from school the next day.

Theo,

   I asked JeeBee to come downtown and pick up letters for you and your mom and Janet. I'm so sorry about yesterday. You took off so fast. I tried to catch up with the bus, but I just missed it.

   I should have written this letter a long, long time ago. I'm sorry.

   That doesn't even begin to cover it. I could fill up this whole letter writing "I'm sorry" over and over. I've done some bad things in my life, but what I did to you and your mom and sister is the worst.

   I wouldn't be surprised if you tore this letter up without even reading it. But I hope you'll give me a chance to try and explain why I haven't been a dad to you in almost five years.

It doesn't mean I haven't loved you and haven't thought about you every single day. You may not believe that, but it's true.

I don't know if this will make sense to you or not, but when I got home from the war, I was too angry to be happy. After what I saw over there — what we _did_ over there — and how our country treated us when we got home. Like we were an embarrassment. Like we'd done something shameful.

I knew you and Janet needed a dad, a whole dad who could help you with your homework and read you stories at bedtime and take you to the park. A dad who would make you feel secure and safe. But I wasn't sure if I could do that.

You deserve for me to at least be honest. I started driving home the same day I got processed out. I bought a junker and headed east. I'd been driving all day across Nevada. It was late afternoon, and it was hot. I started getting too sleepy to drive, so I stopped in a little town. There was a bar at the edge of town and I decided I'd get a sandwich and a cold beer and then find a motel for the night. And then I'd call you.

Inside was this guy. He was drunk and he was being a jerk, but I thought I'd just go down to the end of the bar and ignore him and eat my sandwich and then go. But the drunk wouldn't leave me alone. He must have noticed my haircut, because he figured out I'd been in Vietnam and he kept hassling me. He would not shut up, just hassling me about what a jerk I was for fighting in such a terrible war. I don't even remember exactly what he was saying, only that I wanted him to be quiet, and the next thing I knew, he was lying on the floor and my knuckle was bloody from hitting his teeth.

It wasn't so much that I punched him — that was dumb, but that's not what bothered me. What bothered me was that I don't even remember punching him. I did it without thinking. They kicked me out of the bar and I stood outside with the hot sun beating down, looking at my bloody knuckle and wondering what if I did it again — just decked someone without even being able to control it? It scared me. I didn't want to come home until I was sure that wouldn't happen.

But I couldn't call and say that. Your mom didn't even want me going to Vietnam in the first place. If I called up and told her it had messed me up so bad, well, I just couldn't do that. I didn't want to hear what she'd say. Not that I'm blaming her. I'm the one who did something wrong, not her.

So I wrote and told her I needed a little time. I swear to you I didn't think it would take this long. I thought maybe I could just go off in the woods for a few weeks and walk the anger away. But it didn't work out like that. I moved around a lot. I thought I could figure it all out for myself. It took me a long time to admit that I needed help. Finally in Detroit I started talking to a counselor. We worked together for a long time, until I started feeling better.

The counselor suggested I do some volunteer work with kids, and after a while I started feeling like I could be part of a family again. But I was afraid it might be too late. I thought maybe you'd be better off without me. I found a job in

D.C., just in case. And then I called JeeBee. To find out if you want to see me again.

It's taken your grandma a couple of weeks to convince me that maybe you do. She said you've been asking about me. She showed me the pictures from your birthday. I can't believe how big you're getting. I'm so proud of you, son.

Can I still call you that? It's up to you, Theo. I'll understand if you say no. But maybe you'll give me a chance to start being a little bit of a dad to you. You deserve a better one, and I'm sorry about that.

I don't have to come to the house. I'm not sure your mom would like that. But we could meet somewhere, at the park, maybe. JeeBee could stay with you and Janet the whole time. We could meet for a little while and then you could decide if you want to meet again.

Think about it and let JeeBee know what you want to do.

I'd like to sign this Dad, but I know I have to earn that. I'll just sign this —

*Vince*

When Theo looked up, Mom was standing in the doorway. "You know, it's my fault, really, that he didn't come home." She stepped into the room as far as the desk and sat down on Theo's chair. "I was so mad when he went to war — so mad that he'd go off and leave me all alone to take care of everything: the house and the bills and the car and you and Janet. And I was studying so hard in school. I felt buried in responsibility." She shook her head. "And I never let him forget it — what a burden it was on *me* when he joined the army. How much I had to sacrifice."

She leaned forward, resting her elbows on her knees, and looked at the floor. "I wrote him how hard it was, having him gone, and how lonely I was. But I never really acknowledged —" Mom's voice cracked. She took a deep breath. "I never acknowledged the sacrifice *he* made, how much he had to give up. It killed him to leave you and Janet — he knew he'd miss so much of your growing up." She closed her eyes. "You'd think I could have been a little more generous. You'd think I could have written and told him that."

Mom rubbed her temples with her hands like she was massaging a headache.

"You messed up," Theo said. "You need to fix it."

Mom shook her head. "It's not that simple, Theo."

Theo thought about this. "You don't have to fix it all at once."

Mom searched his eyes. Slowly, she nodded. "You're right." Then she came over to the bed and pulled him into a hug. "I love you so much."

Theo sank into Mom's hug. He thought back to what Mr. Meyer had said — that even if it made Mom cry, Theo could still tell her how he felt. "I don't like how things are at home, how we never talk about Dad. It makes me feel like I'm all by myself."

Mom hugged him harder.

"I want us to talk more."

She kissed the top of his head. "I want that, too."

"And Mom . . . instead of you going into your room, could we read together sometimes?"

Mom laughed, pure joy.

Theo felt himself being rocked back and forth. He closed his eyes. "I wish he had come home."

Theo had cried about Dad before. But this was the first time — with Mom's arms wrapped around him, fiercely murmuring that she loved him, that it was going to be alright — this was the first time he began to feel just a little bit better.

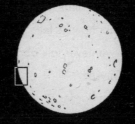

LACUS AESTATIS

# SUMMER LAKE

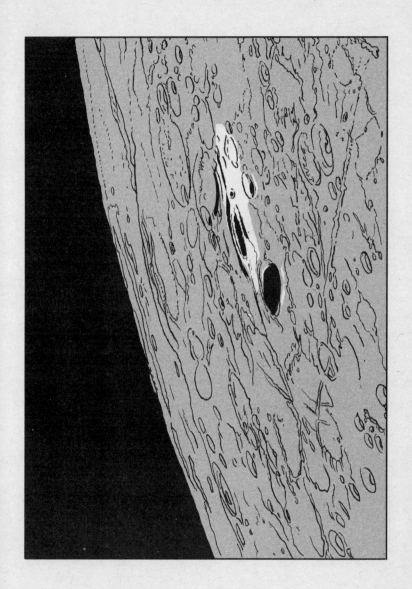

**WHEN THE EAGLE SEPARATED FROM** the command module, it left Mike Collins behind. For the next twenty-eight hours, as Neil and Buzz flew down together to explore the lunar surface, Mike Collins orbited the moon, over and over again. He even got to study the far side of the moon, the side we never get to see.

He talked to Neil and Buzz, and he talked to the guys at Mission Control in Houston. He was in contact with everyone.

Only here's the thing: When he flew behind the moon, he couldn't hear or talk to anyone. The moon blocked out his communications signals. For every two hours it took to orbit the moon, forty-eight minutes of it he was cut off from every other person in the universe. I mean, later he could tell someone what he remembered seeing, but when he was actually flying behind the moon, he was completely alone.

If something had gone wrong with the equipment when he was back there, he wouldn't have been able to tell anyone what happened. Mission Control was full of all these brilliant rocket scientists running all this fancy equipment. But every time Mike Collins went behind the moon, the guys at Mission Control were completely helpless. It didn't matter if they knew every nut and bolt on the whole Saturn 5 rocket—when Mike went behind the moon, the scientists just had to sit there and wait.

Every orbit, they probably held their breath, and the whole control room got really quiet. I bet everyone sat there, worrying and wondering, waiting to welcome him back.

**THEO COULDN'T SLEEP. HE WAS**
down in the kitchen, taking the milk out of the fridge when
Janet walked in, her fuzzy pink slippers scuffing the floor.
She blinked in the kitchen light. "Hey, baby brother. You
want a sandwich?"

She got out the ingredients for peanut-butter-and-
potato-chip sandwiches. She slapped slices of bread onto
the counter. "I can't believe Mom and JeeBee. And Dad.
I can't believe any of this."

"Me, neither." He poured milk into two glasses. Then
he got the syrup out of the fridge to make chocolate milk.

Janet spread peanut butter and heaped potato chips
on top. "You could have told me about the letters, Theo. I
know you think I'm a big blabber, but I can keep a secret
when I need to." She closed up the sandwiches, flatten-
ing each with the palm of her hand.

"I know. I should have told you. I'm sorry. I'll give
them to you tomorrow."

Janet put the sandwiches on plates. "And I guess I
should have told you a long time ago about Dad not
being MIA. Sorry."

Theo shook his head. "We're all a bunch of liars. This whole family." He carried the chocolate milk over to the table.

"I know," Janet said, bringing over the plates. "It's so stupid."

"I'm not going to lie anymore," Theo said. "I'm just going to say whatever I'm thinking."

Janet nodded.

"What did your letter from Dad say?"

Janet let out a deep breath. "He talked about how angry he was after the war, and I kept thinking, yeah, well, I'm angry, too. Then he said he punched some guy in a bar, and he was afraid we'd be scared of him, and I just started thinking . . . how sad it was that he felt like he couldn't come home." Suddenly tears sprang to her eyes. "Theo, he called me Jay-bird. . . . He's the only one who does that." She wiped her eyes on the sleeve of her nightgown. "And now I don't know what to think." She grabbed a napkin and blew her nose. "Sorry." She shook her head. "Eat."

The key to eating peanut-butter-and-potato-chip sandwiches was holding them horizontally. Theo took a crunchy, salty bite. "So, what are you going to do? Do you want to meet him?"

"No." Janet picked up her sandwich, potato chip crumbs raining onto her plate. "Yes. I don't know."

Theo took a big slug of chocolate milk. "I want to meet him."

"You know *already*? How can you be so sure?"

Theo bit into his sandwich again and chewed slowly. "Because he messed up, and now he's trying to fix it."

Janet shook her head. "I don't know what I want to do. It's so confusing."

Theo considered this. "It's like my models — the complicated ones. I think it's only confusing when you try to figure out the whole thing at once."

Janet sat back in her chair, studying his face. "You know," she finally said, "for a baby brother, you're pretty smart." And then, when she saw his surprised expression, added, "Don't let it go to your head, Theodore."

When Theo climbed back into bed later that night, he brought his binoculars with him and focused on the moon. There was Copernicus, landed splat in the Sea of Isles like it had just rolled off the Apennines Mountains. Aristarchus glowed nearby.

Before Galileo, before Copernicus, Aristarchus figured out that Earth revolved around the sun. All these guys looking up at the night sky, asking questions that seemed too big for answers. You could choose any one you wanted, Theo realized, and spend the rest of your life trying to figure it out.

And suddenly, he knew what to do for his *Voyager* project.

Mr. Meyer stood in front of the class, grade book in hand. "Okay, it looks like there are just a few of you who still need to turn in your project." He glanced at Theo. "It's due tomorrow."

When the bell rang, kids shuffled out of their seats. Kenny headed toward the door without a backward glance.

Theo thought about staying after — there was a lot he needed to tell Mr. Meyer. But that would have to wait. He grabbed his books and ran after Kenny.

"Hey!" he said when he caught up to him.

Kenny's stride didn't slow. He fixed his eyes straight forward. "What do you want?"

"I'm sorry," Theo said. "I was a jerk."

Kenny slowed a bit. "Yeah. You were."

"I messed up. I want to fix it," Theo said. "Can you come over? I have a lot I need to tell you."

As they walked to Theo's house, he explained all that had happened. Mostly Kenny listened, interrupting only to ask, "Wait, what?" and "Why did she do that?" and "Were you mad?"

Theo answered as best he could. "And now, he wants to know if we want to meet him."

Kenny shook his head. "Oh, man!"

Theo pushed open the kitchen door. He grabbed a box of cookies from the cupboard and they went up to his room, Janet's stereo blaring from behind her closed door.

"Hey, where are the models?" Kenny asked.

Theo pointed to the trash can full of debris.

Kenny's eyes bugged out. "What happened?"

"I got mad."

"I'll say." Kenny flopped down on the bed.

Just then, Janet walked in. "Theo, I wanted to get —" But then she saw Kenny. "Oh. I'll come back later. . . ."

"It's okay, Janet," Theo said. He retrieved the letters from their hiding place and handed them over. "Kenny knows. I told him everything."

Janet bit her lip. "Oh. That's good. That you have someone to talk to." She smiled at Kenny and then left.

Kenny's eyes grew big. "Was she being *nice* to me?"

Theo grinned. "I think so."

"Wow." He stuck two cookies into his mouth, whole, and chewed for a while. Then he asked, "Hey, did you ever do your *Voyager* thing?"

Theo grinned again. "No, but I figured out what I want to do. You wanna help?"

That afternoon, they took the tape player all around, recording everyone: the librarian, the neighbors, Kenny's parents. Theo even stopped a jogger passing by his house.

He did his friends, his family, everyone. And soon, he had his minute of tape: the librarian's whisper, the jogger's pant, Kenny's goofy squawk, Janet's this-is-so-dumb huff, voice after voice asking, "What do you think is the most important thing about Earth?"

Theo's voice came last on the tape, the same thing he wrote out neatly on a piece of paper for his bulletin board contribution:

WE ASK QUESTIONS

## THERE'S A REASON VOYAGER 2 IS

taking off this summer: The outer planets are all lined up. The gravity from each planet will boost the spacecraft faster than any rocket could. Jupiter's gravity will swing it toward Saturn. Then Saturn's gravity will swing it to Uranus, and then Uranus's to Neptune.

The planets only line up like this every two hundred years. NASA saw the chance and they jumped at it. A once-in-a-lifetime opportunity.

Voyager 2 will study the planet Jupiter, and Galileo's moons. It'll swing by the outer planets. And then in about twenty or thirty years, it'll leave our solar system.

For the next 300,000 years, Voyager 2 will fly toward Sirius, the brightest star in the whole sky. And when it gets there, if we're lucky, someone will play the golden record: a greeting to an alien life-form, hoping he'll listen, hoping he's friendly.

That's kinda what this tape is, too.

# THE NEXT MORNING, THEO SAT

on his bed. He listened to his *Voyager* tape one last time, then turned off the machine.

Copernicus. Galileo. Mercator. Einstein. They all found answers, lots of answers. But they all started by asking questions.

Theo looked around the room. Someone had hung the F-86 Sabre jet with its clumsy yellow stripes back up, flying all by itself. Probably Janet, while he was out making his tape. She'd left the string and scissors on his desk next to his *Saturn 5* rocket.

Theo got up and examined the launch platform. The glue had dried. He could attach the rocket to it tonight.

But now Theo realized that the rocket wouldn't have to sit on the launch platform on his desk, forever earthbound. He cleared away the clutter and placed the launch platform in the corner of the desk. He cut off pieces of string and looped them around the rocket's middle. Then he climbed up on the desk and suspended the rocket over the platform, right as it took off, flying straight up.

He captured the exact moment when it blasted toward space.

Theo climbed down and sat back on his bed, watching the rocket blast skyward. What were the astronauts feeling those first few minutes as the rocket's thrust pressed them back in their seats? Did they feel vibrations? Did their blood rush and pulse in their ears? Did they scream the kind of scream you make on a roller coaster, the kind that comes out even though you don't mean it to?

It would slowly get dark, wouldn't it? Darker and darker out the windows of the rocket as it left the atmosphere and entered space.

Once the rocket blasted off, that was it. You'd be on board for the duration of the ride, no turning back.

No turning back.

Theo popped out his *Voyager* tape and slid in a new, blank one. He pushed the RECORD button. Then he began: *"Mom says I have my head in the clouds, but she's a hundred miles short. . . ."*

# PEOPLE USED TO BELIEVE THE

weather depended on the moon. That's why stuff is named what it is.

There was this old saying that when the moon is waxing, the weather will be nice, and when it's waning, the weather will be rainy. So they gave the eastern side of the moon peaceful names like the Sea of Tranquility and the Lake of Dreams, and the western side stormy names like the Sea of Rains and the Bay of Billows.

But the moon's not divided up completely like that. Some of the names are mixed up together. Guess what's on the shores of the Sea of Serenity: all these mixed-up lakes — Hate and Suffering right next to Tenderness and Joy.

The moon has all these magical, beautiful places. The Sea of Nectar. The Bay of Rainbows. The Bay of Faith.

But the place I most want to go isn't fancy like that. It's just a little place called Summer Lake. It sounds like the kind of place you'd go with your family on the weekend, maybe bring a picnic. Even if every-one had been really busy and you hadn't seen each other all week, you'd take a few hours every weekend and spend it together at Summer Lake.

That's where I most want to go. I'm going to get there one day.

Well, this tape's almost used up. I guess I could get another one and keep talking, but I think this is enough. JeeBee's heading downtown in a little while. I'll give this to her to give to you.

Mom warned me that maybe you won't come tomorrow. She told me not to get my hopes up, that even though you promised JeeBee, you still might not show up.

But I think you will. You've listened this far. This is just the start.

## FOR ONCE JANET AND THEO

hadn't fought over who got the front seat of the car. Janet wanted to sit in back, right up next to JeeBee, holding on to JeeBee.

They turned in to the park. Through his open window, Theo could smell the wet grass.

Mom pulled into the parking lot and turned off the engine.

Down the hill, Theo could see Dad sitting on a picnic table by the duck pond, looking out at the water.

Theo unbuckled his seat belt. "Are you coming?" he asked his mom.

"I can't, Theo. Not yet." She reached over and gave his arm a squeeze. "Maybe next time."

He nodded. "Okay, Mom." Then he turned to the backseat. "Ready?" he asked Janet.

But she just closed her eyes. "I don't know if I can do this."

JeeBee patted Janet's hand. "That's alright, dear, take all the time you need." Then she smiled at Theo. "Why don't you go on ahead?"

Theo opened the car door.

"Theo!" Janet added as he stepped out. "Tell him . . . tell him I'll try, okay?"

Theo nodded and closed the car door. He thrust his hands into his pockets.

Slowly he walked through the wet grass, down to the pond. As he neared the shore, a duck swam toward him. It waddled up to the picnic table and quacked.

Dad laughed, then turned to look over his shoulder. "Theo."

Theo stepped forward. "I knew you'd come."

Dad smiled. "I finished listening to your tape this morning. We have so much catching up to do. I don't even know where to start."

"That's okay." Theo settled on the other end of the picnic table and looked at the pond. Sunlight twinkled on the water. Like stars, he thought. "I'll go first. I have a million questions to ask you."

# SOURCES AND SUGGESTIONS FOR FURTHER READING

The people and events described in Dad's letters, while reflective of many soldiers' experiences in the Vietnam War, are fictitious.

During my research, I drew on many accounts of the war and the Apollo space program. I found *Life* magazine to be especially helpful. The photos and articles described in the novel can be found in the following issues (in order of their appearance in the text):

Bicentennial Issue, 1975; May 14, 1965; May 21, 1965; July 4, 1969; August 8, 1969; June 27, 1969; January 27, 1967; March 10, 1967; January 13, 1967; February 26, 1971; February 9, 1968; February 23, 1968; October 27, 1967; and August 25, 1967. "The 100 Events That Shaped America" appeared in a special-report Bicentennial Issue in 1975. "One Week's Dead" appeared in the June 27, 1969, issue. Profiles of the astronauts appeared in the July 4, 1969, issue.

• • •

I am also indebted to the book *Atlas of the Moon* by Antonín Rükl (Waukesha, Wisconsin Kalmbach Books, 1990) for general information about the moon and its topography.

• • •

To learn more about the Vietnam War and the *Voyager* spacecraft:

## WEB SITES

"American Experience: Vietnam Online"
http://www.pbs.org/wgbh/amex/vietnam
A companion Web site to the public television series, containing information, maps, and photographs of the Vietnam War.

"Veterans History Project"
http://www.loc.gov/vets/vets-home.html
A Library of Congress Web site providing stories and photographs of the veteran experience.

"Vietnam War Resources"
http://www.readwritethink.org/lesson_images/lesson821/vietnam-sites.html
A Web site sponsored by the International Reading Association, the National Council of Teachers of English, and the MarcoPolo Consortium, listing links to many Vietnam War–related sites.

"The Golden Record"

http://voyager.jpl.nasa.gov/spacecraft/goldenrec.html

NASA's Jet Propulsion Laboratory site about the golden record, containing samples of pictures, Earth sounds, and greetings featured on the actual golden record, as well as a list of the music included.

"*Voyager*: The Interstellar Mission"

http://voyager.jpl.nasa.gov

NASA's Jet Propulsion Laboratory site about the *Voyager* spacecraft, containing information on the spacecraft's mission, a multimedia presentation, and a special section just for kids.

# BOOKS

Caputo, Philip. *10,000 Days of Thunder: A History of the Vietnam War* (NEW YORK: ATHENEUM BOOKS FOR YOUNG READERS, 2005). A Pulitzer Prize–winning journalist's account of the Vietnam War, written for young people.

Murray, Stuart. Eyewitness Books: *Vietnam War* (NEW YORK: DK PUBLISHING, INC., 2005). An excellent overview of the war, with many photographs.

# ABOUT THE AUTHOR

Barbara Kerley is the author of several award-winning picture books, including WHAT TO DO ABOUT ALICE?, a Sibert Honor Book, a Boston Globe-Horn Book Honor Book, and an ALA Notable Book; and THE DINOSAURS OF WATERHOUSE HAWKINS, a Caldecott Honor Book and an ALA Notable Book.

About the inspiration for GREETINGS FROM PLANET EARTH, she says, "Ever since I was a kid, I've looked up at the night sky, feeling part of something bigger. I love the idea of the golden record carrying a tiny snapshot of our world out into space. That we're capable of such a hopeful gesture, despite the destructive things we sometimes do, gives me tremendous faith in humanity."

Barbara Kerley lives in Portland, Oregon. You can visit her at www.barbarakerley.com.